ESCAPE!

BEN BOVA

SCHOLASTIC BOOK SERVICES
New York Toronto London Auckland Sydney Tokyo

Copyright © 1970 by Ben Bova. This edition is published
by Scholastic Book Services, a division of Scholastic Maga-
zines, Inc., by arrangement with Holt, Rinehart and Winston.

1st printing .... October 1975
Printed in the U. S. A.

To my parents, with love and gratitude

Chapter One

The door shut behind him.

Danny Romano stood in the middle of the small room, every nerve tight. He listened for the click of the lock. Nothing.

Quiet as a cat, he tiptoed back to the door and tried the knob. It turned. The door was unlocked.

Danny opened the door a crack and peeked out into the hallway. Empty. The guards who had brought him here were gone. No voices. No footsteps. Down at the far end of the hall, up near the ceiling, was some sort of TV camera. A little red light glowed next to its lens.

He shut the door and leaned against it.

"Don't let 'em sucker you," he said to himself. "This is a jail."

Danny looked all around the room. There was only one bed. On its bare mattress was a pile of clothes, bed sheets, towels and stuff. A TV screen was set into the wall at the end of the bed. On the other side of the room was a desk, an empty bookcase, and two stiff-back wooden chairs. Somebody had painted the walls a soft blue.

"This can't be a cell . . . not for me, anyway. They made a mistake."

The room was about the size of the jail cells they always put four guys into. Or sometimes six.

And there was something else funny about it.

1

The smell, that's it! This room smelled clean. There was even fresh air blowing in through the open window. And there were no bars on the window. Danny tried to remember how many jail cells he had been in. Eight? Ten? They had all stunk like rotting garbage.

He went to the clothes on the bed. Slacks, real slacks. Sport shirts and turtlenecks. And colors! Blue, brown, tan. Danny yanked off the gray coveralls he had been wearing, and tried on a light blue turtleneck and dark brown slacks. They even fit right. Nobody had ever been able to find him a prison uniform small enough to fit his wiry frame before this.

Then he crossed to the window and looked outside. He was on the fifth or sixth floor, he guessed. The grounds around the building were starting to turn green with the first touch of early spring. There were still a few patches of snow here and there, in the shadows cast by the other buildings.

There were a dozen buildings, all big and square and new-looking. Ten floors high, each of them, although there were a couple of smaller buildings farther out. One of them had a tall smokestack. The buildings were arranged around a big, open lawn that had cement paths through it. A few young trees lined the walkways. They were just beginning to bud.

"No fences," Danny said to himself.

None of the windows he could see had bars. Everyone seemed to enter or leave the buildings freely. No guards and no locks on the doors? Out past the farthest building was an area of trees. Danny knew from his trip in here, this morning, that beyond the woods was the highway that led back to the city.

Back to Laurie.

Danny smiled. What were the words the judge

had used? *In . . . in-de-ter-minate sentence.* The lawyer had said that it meant he was going to stay in jail for as long as they wanted him to. A year, ten years, fifty years. . . .

"I'll be out of here tonight!" He laughed.

A knock on the door made Danny jump. *Somebody heard me!*

Another knock, louder this time. "Hey, you in there?" a man's voice called.

"Y . . . yeah."

The door popped open. "I'm supposed to talk with you and get you squared away. My name's Joe Tenny."

Joe was at least forty, Danny saw. He was stocky, tough-looking, but smiling. His face was broad; his dark hair combed straight back. He was a head taller than Danny and three times wider. The jacket of his suit looked tight across the middle. His tie was loosened, and his shirt collar unbuttoned.

A cop, Danny thought. *Or maybe a guard. But why ain't he wearing a uniform?*

Joe Tenny stuck out a heavy right hand. Danny didn't move.

"Listen, kid," Tenny said, "we're going to be stuck together for a long time. We might as well be friends."

"I got my own friends," said Danny. "On the outside."

Tenny's eyebrows went up while the corners of his mouth went down. His face seemed to say, *Who are you trying to kid, wise guy?*

Aloud, he said, "Okay, suit yourself. You can have it any way you like, hard or easy." He reached for one of the chairs and pulled it over near the bed.

"How long am I going to be here?"

"That depends on you. A couple of years, at

3

least." Joe turned the chair around backwards and sat on it as if it were a saddle, leaning his stubby arms on the chair's back.

Danny swung at the pile of clothes and things on the bed, knocking most of them onto the floor. Then he plopped down on the mattress. The springs squeaked in complaint.

Joe looked hard at him, then let a smile crack his face. "I know just what's going through your mind. You're thinking that two years here in the Center is going to kill you, so you're going to crash out the first chance you get. Well, for*get* it! The Center is escape-proof."

In spite of himself, Danny laughed.

"I know, I know. . . ." Tenny grinned back at him. "The Center looks more like a college campus than a jail. In fact, that's what most of the kids call it — the campus. But believe me, Alcatraz was easy compared to this place. We don't have many guards or fences, but we've got TV cameras, and laser alarms, and SPECS."

"Who's Specks?" Danny asked.

Joe called out, "SPECS, say hello."

The TV screen on the wall lit up. A flat, calm voice said, "GOOD MORNING DR. TENNY. GOOD MORNING MR. ROMANO. WELCOME TO THE JUVENILE HEALTH CENTER."

Danny felt totally confused. Somebody was talking through the TV set? The screen, though, showed the words he was hearing, spelled out a line at a time. But they moved too fast for Danny to really read them. And Specks, whoever he was, called Joe Tenny a doctor.

"Morning SPECS," Tenny said to the screen. "How's it going today?"

"ALL SYSTEMS ARE FUNCTIONING WELL, DR. TENNY. A LIGHT TUBE IN CORRIDOR SIX OF BUILDING NINE BURNED OUT DURING THE NIGHT. I HAVE

4

REPORTED THIS TO THE MAINTENANCE CREW. THEY WILL REPLACE IT BEFORE LUNCH. THE MORNING CLASSES ARE IN PROGRESS. ATTENDANCE IS . . ."

"Enough, skip the details." Joe turned back to Danny. "If I let him, he'd give me a report on every stick and stone in the Center."

"Who is he?" Danny asked.

"Not a *he,* really. An *it.* A computer. Special Computer System. Take the 's-p-e' from 'special' and the 'c' and 's' from 'computer system' and put the letters together: SPECS. He runs most of the Center. Sees all and knows all. And he never sleeps."

"Big deal," said Danny, trying to make it sound tough.

Joe Tenny turned back to the TV screen, which was still glowing. "SPECS, give me Danny Romano's record, please."

The reply came without an instant's wait: "DANIEL FRANCIS ROMANO. AGE SIXTEEN. HEIGHT FIVE FEET SIX INCHES. WEIGHT ONE HUNDRED TWENTY-SIX POUNDS. SENTENCED TO INDETERMINATE SENTENCE IN THE JUVENILE HEALTH CENTER. FOUND GUILTY OF ATTEMPTED MURDER, RIOTING, LOOTING, ATTACKING A POLICE OFFICER WITH A DEADLY WEAPON, RESISTING ARREST. EARLIER CONVICTIONS INCLUDE PETTY THEFT, AUTOMOBILE THEFT, ASSAULT AND BATTERY, RESISTING ARREST, VANDALISM. SERVED SIX MONTHS IN STATE PRISON FOR BOYS. ESCAPED AND RECAPTURED . . ."

"That's enough," Joe said. "Bad scene, isn't it?"

"So?"

"So it's why you're here."

Danny asked, "What kind of place is this? How come I'm not in a regular jail?"

Joe thought a minute before answering. "This

is a new place. This Center has been set up for kids like you. Kids who are going to kill somebody — or get themselves killed — unless we can change them. Our job is to help you to change. We think you can straighten out. There's no need for you to spend the rest of your life in trouble and in jail. But you've got to let us help you. And you've got to help yourself."

"How . . . how long will I have to stay here?"

Tenny's face turned grim. "Like I said, a couple of years, at least. But it really depends on you. You're going to stay as long as it takes. If you don't shape up, you stay. It's that simple."

Chapter Two

Joe Tenny went right on talking. He used SPECS' TV screen to show Danny a map of the Center and the layouts of the different buildings. He pointed out the classrooms, the cafeteria, the gym and shops, and game rooms.

But Danny didn't see any of it, didn't hear a single word. All he could think of was: *as long as it takes. If you don't shape up, you stay.*

They were going to keep him here forever. Danny knew it. Tenny was a liar. They were all liars. Like that lousy social worker when he was a kid. She told him they were sending him to a special school. "It's for your own good, Daniel." Good, real good. Some school. No teachers, no books. Just guards who belted you when they felt like it, and guys who socked you when the guards weren't looking.

If you don't shape up, you stay. Shape up to what? Get a job? How? Where? Who would hire a punk sixteen-year-old who's already spent half his life in jails?

"We gave you a good room," Joe said, getting up suddenly from his chair. "Your building's right next-door to the cafeteria."

Danny snapped his attention back to the real world.

"Come on, it's just about lunchtime."

7

He followed Joe Tenny out into the hallway, to the elevator, and down to the ground floor of the building. Danny saw that somebody had scratched his initials on the metal inner door of the elevator, and somebody else had worked very hard to erase the scratches. They were barely visible.

They pushed through the glass doors and followed a cement walkway across the piece of lawn that separated the two buildings. Danny shivered in the sudden chill of the outside air. Tenny walked briskly, like he was in a hurry.

Groups of boys — two, three, six, eight in a bunch — were walking across the campus grounds toward the cafeteria building. They were talking back and forth, joking, horsing around.

But Danny's mind was still racing. *I can't stay here. Can't leave Laurie alone on the outside. Some other guy will grab her. By the time I get out, she won't even remember me. Got to get out fast!*

Joe pushed open the glass doors of the cafeteria building. It was warm inside, and noisy. And it smelled of cooking.

"DR. TENNY," called a loudspeaker. Danny thought it sounded like SPECS' voice only much louder and with a bit of an echo to it. "DR. TENNY, PLEASE REPORT TO THE ADMINISTRATION BUILDING."

"Looks like I miss lunch," Joe said, glancing up at the loudspeaker. Danny saw that it was set into the panelled ceiling. There was a TV lens with its unblinking red eye next to it, watching them.

"Have a good feed, Danny. The rest of the day's all yours. Move around, make some friends. SPECS will get you up at the right time tomorrow morning and tell you which classes to go to. See you!"

And with a wave of a heavy, thick-wristed

8

hand, Joe headed back for the glass doors and outside.

Danny watched him go. Then a half-dozen boys pushed through the doors and walked in toward the cafeteria. They were laughing and wise-cracking among themselves. No one said hello or seemed to notice Danny at all.

Turning, Danny headed for the food. Around a corner of the hallway was a big, open, double doorway. Inside it was the cafeteria, noisy and busy with at least a hundred boys. They were standing in line, waving across the big room to friends, rushing toward tables with trays of steaming food, talking, laughing, eating. They moved as freely as they wanted and they all seemed to be talking as loudly as their lungs would let them.

The tables were small, four or six places each. In a few spots, boys had pushed together a couple of tables to make room for a bigger group.

Danny remembered the dining room in the State Prison. You marched in single file and ate at long, wooden tables that were so old the paint was gone. The wood itself was cracked and carved with the initials of fifty years' worth of boys.

This cafeteria was sparkling new. The walls, the tables, the floors all gleamed with fresh paint and plastic and metal. One whole wall was glass. Outside you could see a stretch of grass and a few young trees.

He took a place at the end of the food line. The boys moved along quickly, even though some of them were talking and kidding back and forth. Soon Danny was taking a tray and a wrapped package of spoon, knife, and fork. All plastic.

It surprised him to see that there were no people behind the food counter. Everything was automatic. Boys took a bowl of soup, or a sandwich, or a metal-foil dish that held an entire hot dinner in it. As soon as one piece was taken, another popped through a little door in the wall to replace it.

"You're new here, aren't you?"

Danny turned to see, in line behind him, a tall boy with sandy hair and a scattering of freckles across his snub nose.

"My name's Alan Peterson. No, don't tell me yours. Let me see if I can remember it. SPECS flashed pictures of all the new guys on the news this morning. You're . . . emm . . . Danny something-or-other. Right?"

"Danny Romano."

Alan grinned. "See, I got it. Almost."

"Yeah." Danny reached for a sandwich and an apple. The only drinks he could see were milk, either white or chocolate. He took a chocolate.

Stepping away, Danny looked around for a table.

"Come on with me," Alan said cheerfully. "I'll sit you down with some of the guys. You ought to make friends."

Alan steered him toward a six-place table. Three of the seats were already filled. Danny stopped suddenly.

"I ain't sittin' there."

"Why not?"

Danny jerked his head toward one of the boys at the table. " 'Cause I don't eat with niggers, that's why not."

Chapter Three

Alan looked at Danny in a funny way. Not sore, but almost.

"Okay," he said softly. "Find your own friends."

He left Danny standing there with the tray in his hands and went to the table. Another Negro came up at the same time and sat beside Alan.

Danny found a small table that was empty and sat there alone, with his back to the doors and the food line. He was facing the glass wall and the outside.

He ate quickly, thinking, *Don't waste any time. Walk around, see how big the place is, how hard it'll be to get out.*

He got up from the table and started to walk away. But SPECS' voice came from an overhead loudspeaker:

"PLEASE TAKE YOUR TRAY TO THE DISPOSAL SLOT IF YOU ARE FINISHED EATING. THANK YOU."

Danny looked up at the ceiling, then turned and saw other boys bringing their trays to a slot in the wall, not far from the table where he was. With a small shrug, he took his tray to the slot.

He watches everything, Danny thought as he glanced up at one of the TV cameras in the ceiling.

It was still chilly outside after lunch, even though the sun was shining. Danny thought he

11

had seen a jacket — a windbreaker — among the clothes on his bed. But he didn't bother going back to his room. Instead, he jammed his fists in his slacks pockets, hunched his shoulders, and headed toward the trees that were out at the edge of the campus.

He didn't get far.

From behind him, a soft voice said, "Here you don't like eatin' with black men, skinny."

Danny turned around. Two Negroes were standing there, grinning at him. But there was no friendship in their smiles. Danny thought they might be the two boys who had been at the table Alan tried to steer him to.

For a moment they just stood there, looking each other over. There were a couple of other boys around, white and black, but they stayed a little distance away. Out of it. Danny could feel himself tensing, his fists clenching hard inside his pockets.

One of the blacks was Danny's own height, and not much heavier. The other was tall and thin, built for basketball. He had sleepy-looking eyes, and a bored, cool look on his face.

"That true, skinny?" the tall one asked. "You don't want to eat with us?"

Danny swore at him.

"My, my, such language," said the smaller of them. "Real rough one, this guy. Hard as nails."

"Yeah . . . fingernails."

They both laughed. Danny said nothing.

The tall Negro said slowly, "Listen baby. You got a problem. You're bein' put down in the schedule to fight Lacey here, first of the month."

Lacey nodded and grinned brightly. "So start workin' out in the gym, Whitey, or you won't last even half a round."

12

"Yeah." The tall one added, "And in case you don't know it, Lacey here's the lightweight champ o' this whole Center. And he ain't gonna be playing games with you in that ring. Dig?"

And they both walked away, as quickly and softly as they had come. Danny stood there alone, trembling with rage. He was so angry that his chest was starting to hurt.

The other boys who had been hanging around, started to drift back toward the buildings. But one of the white boys came up to Danny.

"My name's Ralph Malzone. I seen what them black bastards done to ya."

Ralph was a big redhead, huge and solid, like a pro-football player. His face was round and puffy, with tiny eyes squinting out, and little round ears plastered flat against his skull. He looked as if his skin was stretched as tight as it could go, another ounce would split it apart. But Ralph didn't look fat; he looked *hard*.

Danny looked up at him. "I couldn't even understand what they were saying, half the time."

"I heard 'em," Ralph answered. "You're new, huh? Well, there's a boxing match here every month. You been put down to fight Lacey. He's the lightweight champ. If you don't fight him, everybody'll think you're chicken."

Danny didn't answer. He just stood there, feeling cold whenever the wind gusted by.

"Lacey's fast. Hits hard for a little guy."

"I'm shaking," Danny said.

Ralph laughed. "Hey, you're okay. Listen, I'll help you out. In the gym. I know a lot about fighting."

"Why should you help me?"

Ralph's face started to look mean. "I don't like to see white guys gettin' picked on. And I want

13

that Lacey creamed. He needs his head busted. Only, they won't let me fight him. I'm a heavyweight."

Grinning, Danny asked, "Why wait for the first of the month? Get him outside."

"Boy, wouldn't I like to!" Ralph said. "But it ain't as easy as it sounds. Too many TV cameras around. Step out of line and they catch you right away. . . . But you got the right idea. Boy, I'd *love* to mash that little crumb."

Nodding, Danny said, "Okay . . . uh, I'll see you in the gym sometime."

"Good," said Ralph. "I'll look for you."

Chapter Four

Ralph headed back for one of the class-room buildings. Danny started out again for the trees.

It was colder in the woods. The bare branches of the trees seemed to filter out almost all of the sun's warmth. They sky had turned a sort of milky-gray. The ground under Danny's sneakers was damp and slippery from melted snow and the remains of last year's fallen leaves.

Danny hated the cold, hated the woods, hated everything and everybody except the few blocks of city street where he had lived and the guys who had grown up on those streets with him. They were the only guys in the world you could trust. Can't trust grown-ups. Can't trust teachers or cops or lawyers or judges or jail guards. Can't trust Tenny. Can't even trust this new guy, Ralph. Just your own guys, the guys you really know. And Laurie. He had to get back to Laurie.

His feet were cold and wet and he could feel his chest getting tight, making it hard to breathe. Soon his chest would be too heavy to lift, and he'd have to stop walking and wait for his breathing to become normal again. But Danny kept going, puffing little breaths of steam from his mouth as he trudged through the woods.

And there it was!

The fence. A ten-foot-high wire fence. And on the other side of it, the highway. The outside world, with cars zipping by and big trailer trucks shifting gears with a grinding noise as they climbed the hill.

Danny stood at the edge of the trees, a dozen feet from the fence. Two hours down that highway was home. And Laurie.

He leaned his back against a tree, breathing hard, feeling the rough wood through his thin shirt. He listened to himself wheezing. *Like an old man,* he told himself angrily. *You sound like a stupid old man.*

When his breathing became normal again, Danny started walking along the fence. But he stayed in among the trees, so that he couldn't be seen too easily.

No guards. The fence was just a regular wire fence, the kind he'd been able to climb since he was in grade school. There wasn't even any barbed wire at the top. And nobody around to watch.

He could scramble over the fence and hitch a ride back to the city. He wasn't even wearing a prison uniform!

Danny laughed to himself. Why wait? He stepped out toward the fence.

"Hold it Danny! Hold it right there!"

Chapter Five

Danny spun around. Standing there among the trees was Joe Tenny, grinning broadly at him.

"Did you ever stop to think that the fence might be carrying ten thousand volts of electricity?" Joe asked.

Danny's mouth dropped open. Without thinking about it, he took a step back from the fence.

Joe walked past him and reached a hand out to the wire fence. "Relax. It's not 'hot.' We wouldn't want anybody to get hurt."

Danny felt his chest tighten up again. Suddenly it was so hard to breathe that he could hardly talk. "How . . . how'd you . . . know . . . ?"

"I told you the Center was escape-proof. SPECS has been watching you every step of the way. You crossed at least eight different alarm lines. . . . No, you can't see them. But they're there. SPECS called me as soon as you started out through the woods. I hustled down here to stop you."

He's big but he's old, Danny thought. *Getting fat. If I can knock him down and get across the fence . . .*

"Okay, come on back now," Joe was saying.

Danny aimed a savage kick below Joe's belt. But it never landed. Instead he felt himself swept up, saw the highway and then the cloudy sky flash past his eyes, and then landed face-down on the damp grass. Hard.

"For*get* it, kid," Joe said from somewhere above him. "You're too small and I'm too good a wrestler. I'm part Turk, you know."

Danny tried to get up. He tried to get his knees under his body and push himself off the ground. But he couldn't breathe, couldn't move. Everything was black, smelled of wet leaves. He was choking. . . .

He opened his eyes and saw a green curtain in front of him. Blinking, Danny slowly realized that he was in a hospital bed. It was cranked up to a sitting position.

Joe Tenny was sitting beside the bed, his face very serious.

"You okay?" Joe asked.

Danny nodded. "Yeah . . . I think so. . . ."

"You scared me! I thought I had really hurt you. The doctors say it's asthma. How long have you had it?"

"Had what?"

Joe pulled his chair up closer. "Asthma. How long have you had trouble breathing?"

Danny took a deep breath. His chest felt okay again. Better than okay. It had never felt this good.

"It comes and goes," he said. "Hits when I'm working hard . . . running . . . things like that."

"And not a sign of it showed up in your physical exams," Joe muttered. "How old were you when it first hit you?"

"I don't know. What difference does it make?"

"How old?" Joe repeated. His voice wasn't any louder, but it somehow seemed ten times stronger than before.

Danny turned his head away from Joe's intense stare. "Five, maybe six." Then he remembered.

"It was the year my father died. I was five."

Joe grunted. "Okay. The doctors need to know."

"I thought you was a doctor," Danny said, turning back to him.

Tenny smiled. "I am, but not a medical doctor. I'm a doctor of engineering. Been a teacher a good part of my life."

"Oh. . . ."

"You don't think much of teachers? Well, I don't blame you much."

Joe got up from his chair.

Danny looked around. The bed was screened off on three sides by the green curtain. The fourth side, the head of the bed, was against a wall.

"Where am I? How long I been here?" he asked.

"In the Center's hospital. You've been here about six hours. It's past dinnertime."

"I figured I'd be back home by now," Danny mumbled.

Joe looked down at him. "You've had a rough first day. But you've made it rough on yourself. Listen . . . there's a lot I could tell you about the Center. But I think it's better for you to find out things for yourself. All I want you to understand right now is one thing: around here, you'll get what you earn. Understand that? For the first time in your life, you're going to get *exactly* what you earn."

Danny frowned.

"It works both ways," Joe went on. "Make life rough for yourself and you'll earn trouble. Work hard, and you'll earn yourself an open door to the outside. You're the only one who can open that door. It's up to you."

"Sure."

"I mean it. I know you don't believe it, but you

can trust me. You're going to learn that, in time. You don't trust anybody, that's one of the reasons why you're here. . . ."

Danny snapped, "I'm here because I nearly killed a fat-bellied cop in a riot that some niggers started!"

"*Wrong!* You're here because the staff of this Center decided there's a chance we might be able to help you. Otherwise you'd be in a *real* jail."

"What d'ya mean . . . ?"

Joe grabbed the chair again and sat on it. "Why do you think we call this the Juvenile *Health* Center? Because you're sick. All the kids here are sick, one way or another. You come from a sick city, a sick block. Maybe it's not all your fault that you're the way you are, but nobody's going to be able to make you well — nobody! Only you can do that. We're here to help, but we can't do much unless you work to help yourself."

Danny mumbled some street words.

"I understand that," Joe said, his eyes narrowing. "I'm part Sicilian, you know."

"You know everything, huh?"

"Wrong. But I know a lot more than you do. I even know more about Danny Romano than you do. I know there's enough in you to make a solid man. You've got to learn how to become a whole human being, though. My job is to help you do that."

Chapter Six

It was lunchtime the next day before the doctors would let Danny go. He walked across the campus slowly. It was a warmer day, bright with sunshine, and Danny felt pretty good.

Then he remembered that he had failed to escape. He was trapped here at the Center.

"For a while," he told himself. "Not for long, just for a while. Until I figure out how to get around those alarms . . . whatever they are."

He had lunch alone in the crowded, noisy cafeteria. He sat at the smallest table he could find, in a corner by the glass wall. He saw Lacey walk by with a group of Negroes, laughing and clowning around.

Danny finished eating quickly and decided to find the gym. He didn't have to look far. Just outside the cafeteria door was a big overhead sign with an arrow: ELEVATOR TO LIBRARY, POOL, GAME ROOMS, GYM.

He walked down the hall toward the elevator. Other boys were going the same way, some of them hurrying to get into the elevator before it filled up. Danny squeezed in just as the doors slid shut.

"FLOORS PLEASE." It was SPECS' voice.

"Gym," somebody said.

"Library."

"Pool."

"Hey Lou, you goin' swimmin' *again?*"

"It beats takin' a bath!"

Everybody in the elevator laughed.

The gym was on the top floor. The elevator door slid open and a burst of noise and smells and action hit Danny. A basketball game was in full swing. Boys shouting, ball pounding the floorboards, referee blasting on his whistle. Overhead, on a catwalk that went completely around the huge room, other boys were jogging and sprinting, their gray gym suits turning dark with sweat.

But at the far end of the gym was the thing that struck Danny the hardest. A boxing ring. And in it, Lacey was sparring with another black boy.

Danny stood by the elevator and watched, all the sights and sounds and odors of the gym fading away into nothing as he focused every nerve in his body on Lacey.

The guy was good. He moved around the ring like he was gliding on ice skates. His left snapped hard, jerking the other guy's head back when it landed. Then he winged a right across the other guy's guard and knocked him over backwards onto his back.

Turning, Lacey spotted Danny and waved. His black body was gleaming with sweat. His face was one enormous smile, made toothless by the rubber protector that filled his mouth.

"Hello, Danny."

Turning, he saw Alan Peterson standing beside him.

"Hi."

"Watching the champ? I hear you're scheduled to fight him the first of the month."

22

"Yeah." Danny kept his eyes on Lacey. A new sparring partner had come into the ring now. Lacey was jab-jab-jabbing him to death.

"Were you in the hospital yesterday?" Alan asked. "There's a story going around. . . ."

"Yeah, I was." Danny still watched Lacey.

"Are you sick? I mean, will you miss the fight? You can't fight anybody if you're sick."

"I ain't sick."

"But. . . ."

Lacey floored his new partner, this time with a left hook.

"I ain't sick!" Danny snapped. "I'll fight him the first of the month!"

"Okay, don't get sore," said Alan. "It's your funeral."

The loudspeaker suddenly cut through all the noise of the gym: "DANIEL FRANCIS ROMANO, PLEASE REPORT TO DR. TENNY'S OFFICE AT ONCE."

Danny felt almost relieved. He didn't want to hang around the gym any more, but he didn't want Lacey to see him back away. Now he had an excuse to go.

"I'll take you," Alan offered.

Danny said, "I can find it by myself."

Chapter Seven

He had to ask directions once he was outside on the campus. Finally, Danny found the building that the boys called "the front office." It was smaller than the other buildings, only three stories high. The sign over the main door said ADMINISTRATION. Danny wasn't quite sure he knew what it meant.

Inside the door was a sort of a counter, with a girl sitting at a telephone switchboard behind it. She was getting old, Danny saw. Way over thirty, at least. She was reading a paperback book and munching an apple.

"Where's Joe Tenny's office?" Danny asked her.

She swallowed a bite of apple. "*Dr*. Tenny's office is the first door on your left."

Danny went down the hallway that she had pointed to. The first door on the left was marked: DR. J. TENNY, DIRECTOR.

Instead of knocking, he walked back to the switchboard girl. She was bent over her book again, her back to Danny. He noticed for the first time that there was a clear plastic shield between the top of the counter and the ceiling. Like bullet-proof glass. He tapped it.

The girl jumped, surprised, and nearly dropped the book out of her lap.

"Hey," Danny asked, "is Tenny the boss of this whole place?"

She looked very annoyed. "This Center was Dr. Tenny's idea. He fought to get it started and he fought to make it the way it is. Of course he runs it."

"Oh. . . . Uh, thanks."

Danny went back and knocked at Joe's door.

"Come in!"

Joe's office was smaller than Danny's room. It was crammed with papers. Papers covered his desk, the table behind the desk, and lapped over the edges of the bookshelves that filled one whole wall. In a far corner stood an easel with a half-finished painting propped up on it. Brushes and tubes of paint were scattered on the floor beside the easel.

Joe leaned back in his chair. He squinted through the harsh-smelling smoke from the stubby cigar that was clamped in his teeth.

"How're you feeling?"

"Okay."

"Sit down. The smoke bother you?"

"No, it's okay." Danny saw that there was only one other chair in the office, over by the half-open window.

Sitting in it, he asked, "Uh . . . did you tell any of the other guys about, eh, what happened yesterday?"

"About you trying to escape?" Joe shook his head. "No, that's no business of anybody else's. SPECS knows it, of course. But I've ordered SPECS to hold the information as private. Only the staff people who work on your case will be able to learn about it. None of the kids."

Danny nodded.

"Quite a few people saw me carrying you into the hospital, though."

"Yeah . . . I guess so."

Joe tapped the ash off his cigar into the waste-basket next to his desk. "Listen. You're going to start classes tomorrow. Most of the kids spend their mornings studying, and use the afternoons for different things. You're expected to work a couple of hours each afternoon. You can work in one of the shops, or join the repair gang, or something else. Everybody works at something to help keep the Center shipshape. Otherwise the place would fall apart."

Danny frowned. "You mean it's like a job?"

"Right," said Joe, with a grin. "Don't look so glum. It won't hurt you. You get credit for every hour you work, and you can buy things in the Center's store. SPECS runs the store and keeps track of the credits. And it's only a couple hours a day. Then the rest of the day's all yours."

"A job," Danny muttered.

"You can learn a lot from some honest work. And you'll be helping to keep the Center looking neat. You might even get to like it."

"Don't bet on it."

Joe made a sour face. "Okay, I'm not here to argue with you. You have a visitor. She's in the next room."

"She? Laurie?"

Nodding, Joe said, "You can spend the rest of the afternoon with her. But she's got to leave at five."

Without another word, Danny hurried from Dr. Tenny's office and burst into the next room. Laurie was sitting on the edge of a big leather chair. She jumped up and ran into his arms.

After a few minutes, Danny pulled away from her and closed the door.

"How are you?" They both said it at the same time. They laughed.

27

Laurie was a little thinner than Danny remembered her. And sort of pale. She was a small girl, almost frail-looking, with hair and eyes as dark as Danny's own. Danny knew prettier girls, but no one like Laurie. Of all the people in the world, she was the only one that needed Danny. And the only one that he needed.

"You look good," she said.

"You look great."

"Are they treating you okay?"

He nodded. "Sure. Fine. This is more like a school than a jail. How about you? Everything okay?"

"Uh-huh."

They moved slowly to the couch, by the room's only window.

"How's Silvio and the other guys?" Danny asked as they sat down.

"They're all right. . . . Danny, are you really okay?"

Laughing, he said, "Sure. I told you. This ain't really a jail. I nearly broke out of here yesterday. Looks easy. Hardly any guards. I'll probably be out in a couple weeks. Soon's I figure out a couple things."

Laurie's eyes widened. She looked frightened. "Danny, don't do anything they can catch you on. If you get into more trouble. . . ."

"You feel like waitin' around for five years?" he snapped. "Or ten? Twenty? If I can break out, I'm goin' to do it. Reason the other guys don't try it is 'cause they're too soft. They got it too easy here, so they stay. Not me!"

"But they'll just hunt you down again and bring you back. Or maybe put you in a worse place. . . ."

"You *want* me to stay?"

"No. I mean. . . ."

"Listen, I got it figured," Danny said. "Soon's I get out, we grab a car and get up to Canada. Then they can't touch us."

Laurie just looked scared. "All the way to Canada?"

"Just the two of us. We can start all over again. I'll even get a job. . . ."

"Me, too," Laurie said. Then she started to say something else, stopped, and finally said, "Oh, Danny . . . I wanted to tell you. I got a job now. I'm helping my sister in the restaurant where she works. . . ."

"Waiting on tables?" Danny felt his face twist into a frown.

Laurie nodded. Her voice was very low. "And . . . cleaning up, helping in the kitchen."

"I don't want my girl doin' that kind of work!"

"Well, I need some money. . . ." She looked away from him, out toward the window. "I want to be able to live on my own. And the bus to come here costs money."

Danny's frown melted. But he didn't feel any better.

Laurie went on, "Dr. Tenny said I could come once a week, if I wanted to. And he said he thought you could do real good here. Maybe get out in two years."

"I'll be out in a couple weeks," said Danny.

"Please . . . don't do anything they'll catch you on."

"I'll be out in a couple weeks," Danny repeated.

Chapter Eight

Laurie left at five. Danny went over to the cafeteria and picked at his dinner.

Ralph Malzone pulled up a chair and sat beside Danny. He looked much too big for the thin-legged plastic chair.

"Hey, I heard you was sick yesterday. Not going to back out of the fight with Lacey, are ya?"

Danny pushed his tray of food away. "No, I'll fight him."

"Good," said Ralph. He leaned across, took a slice of bread from Danny's tray, and started buttering it. "C'mon over to the gym tomorrow afternoon. I'll show you some tricks. Help make you the new lightweight champ."

Nodding, Danny said, "Sure."

Danny got up to leave. Ralph was still picking food from his tray, so Danny left it there with him.

When he got back to his room and shut the door, the lights turned on and the TV screen lit up.

"GOOD EVENING, MR. ROMANO," said SPECS. The screen spelled out the words.

"How'd you know I was in here?" Danny asked, stopping suddenly by the door and frowning at the screen.

"THERE IS A SENSING DEVICE IN THE DOORWAY.

AND THE ROOM LIGHTS WENT ON. I HAVE A. . . ."

"But how'd you know it was me? Can you see me?"

"THERE ARE NO CAMERAS IN THE STUDENTS' ROOMS. I DID NOT KNOW FOR CERTAIN THAT IT WAS YOU. HOWEVER, THE CHANCES WERE BETTER THAN NINETY PERCENT THAT ONLY YOU WOULD ENTER YOUR OWN ROOM AT THIS TIME OF THE EVENING. I HAVE A MES. . . ."

"Well then, how'd you know I'm Danny Romano? I could of been anybody."

SPECS' voice did not change a bit, but somehow Danny felt that the computer was getting sore at him. "YOUR VOICE IS THE VOICE OF DANIEL FRANCIS ROMANO, AND NO ONE ELSE'S. I HAVE A MESSAGE. . . ."

"You know everybody's voice?"

"I AM PROGRAMED TO RECOGNIZE THE SPEECH PATTERNS AND VOCAL TONES OF EVERYONE IN THE CENTER. I HAVE A MESSAGE FOR YOU FROM THE MEDICAL DEPARTMENT."

SPECS waited patiently for Danny to reply. Finally, Danny said, "Okay, what's the message?"

"YOU WILL FIND A BOTTLE OF PILLS ON THE TABLE BY YOUR BED. THEY ARE FOR ASTHMA. DIRECTIONS ARE WRITTEN ON THE LABEL. THEY READ AS FOLLOWS: 'TAKE ONE PILL BEFORE GOING TO BED AT NIGHT, AND A PILL WHENEVER NEEDED DURING THE DAY. KEEP THIS BOTTLE WITH YOU AT ALL TIMES. NOTIFY THE MEDICAL DEPARTMENT WHEN ONLY FIVE PILLS ARE LEFT.'"

"These pills'll make me breathe okay?"

"I DO NOT HAVE THAT INFORMATION. I CAN PUT YOU IN CONTACT WITH THE MEDICAL DEPARTMENT. DR. MAKOWITZ IS ON DUTY AT THE MOMENT."

"Naw, that's okay."

Danny went to the bed and saw the bottle of

pills on the bed table. They were white, plain-looking. He glanced up at the TV screen and saw that it had gone dead.

"Hey SPECS."

The screen glowed again. "YES, MR. ROMANO?"

"Uh . . . any other messages for me?" Suddenly Danny felt foolish, talking to a TV screen.

"NO OTHER MESSAGES. I HAVE YOUR SCHEDULE FOR TOMORROW'S CLASSES, BUT I AM PROGRAMED TO GIVE THIS INFORMATION TO YOU TOMORROW MORNING, AFTER YOU AWAKEN."

"Can you give it to me now?"

"IF YOU ORDER THE INFORMATION, I AM PRO-GRAMED TO ANSWER YOUR REQUEST."

"You mean if I tell you to do it, you'll do it?"

"YES."

"Suppose I tell you to turn off all the alarms in the Center?"

"I AM NOT PROGRAMED TO ANSWER THAT RE-QUEST."

Danny plopped down on the bed, his mind running fast.

"Listen SPECS. Who can give you orders about the alarms? Who can make you turn 'em off?"

The answer came at once. "DR. TENNY, THE CAPTAIN OF THE GUARDS, THE HIGHEST RANKING MEMBER OF THE GUARDS WHO IS ON DUTY, THE CHIEF OF THE MAINTENANCE DEPARTMENT, THE HIGHEST RANKING MEMBER OF THE MAINTENANCE DEPARTMENT WHO IS ON DUTY."

Danny thought for a moment. "Suppose the guard captain told you right now to turn off all the alarms. Could you do that?"

"YES."

"Okay SPECS," Danny suddenly said loud and firm, "turn off all the alarms!"

"I AM NOT PROGRAMED TO ANSWER THAT RE-QUEST."

"This is the captain of the guards. I order you to turn off all the alarms!"

Danny could have sworn that SPECS was ready to laugh at him. "YOU ARE NOT THE CAPTAIN OF THE GUARD FORCE. YOU ARE DANIEL FRANCIS ROMANO. YOUR VOICE INDEX SHOWS IT."

"Okay SPECS. You got me cold."

"I DO NOT UNDERSTAND THAT STATEMENT."

"You won't tell Tenny about this, will you?"

"THIS CONVERSATION IS RECORDED IN MY MEMORY BANK. IF DR. TENNY OR ANOTHER STAFF MEMBER ASKS TO REVIEW IT, I AM PROGRAMED TO ANSWER THAT REQUEST."

"But you won't tell 'em unless they ask?"

"CORRECT."

Danny grinned. *Tenny can't ask for something unless he knows it exists.*

"Okay. G'night SPECS."

"GOOD NIGHT, MR. ROMANO."

As Danny undressed, he wondered to himself, *Now, where can I get a tape recorder? And maybe I ought to get a gun, too . . . just in case.*

Chapter Nine

When Danny got to his first class the next morning, he thought he was in the wrong room.

It didn't look like a classroom. There were nine other boys already there, sitting around in chairs that were scattered across the floor. A man of about thirty or so was sitting among them, and they were talking back and forth.

"Come on in and take a seat," the teacher said. "My name is Cochran. Be with you in a minute."

Mr. Cochran looked trim and wiry. His hair was clipped very short, like a military crewcut. His back was rifle-straight. He looked to Danny more like a Marine in civilian clothes than a teacher.

Danny picked a seat toward the back of the room. On one side of him the wall was lined with windows. On the other was a row of bookshelves, like a library. There was a big TV screen at the front of the room.

Turning around in his chair, Danny saw that the back of the room was filled with a row of little booths. They looked about the size of telephone booths. Maybe a bit bigger. They were dark inside.

"Hello. You're Daniel Romano?" Mr. Cochran pulled up one of the empty chairs and sat next to Danny. The other boys were reading or writing, or pulling books from the shelves.

"This is a reading class," Cochran explained.

"Different boys are working on different books. I'd like you to start out today on this one."

For the first time, Danny saw that the teacher had a book in his hands. The title was *Friends in the City*.

Danny took the book and thumbed through it. It was filled with pictures of smiling people — grocers, cops, firemen, housewives — living in a clean, bright city.

"You got to be kidding!" He handed the book back to Mr. Cochran.

The teacher grinned. "I know. It's kid stuff. If you think it's too easy for you we can go on to something better. But first you'll have to take a test to see if you're ready for harder work."

He walked Danny back to one of the booths. Opening the door, Mr. Cochran stepped inside and flicked on the lights. Danny saw that the booth had a little desk in it, and the desk was covered with dials and push-buttons. Just above the desk, on the wall of the booth, was a small TV screen.

Mr. Cochran fiddled with the dials and buttons for a few moments, then stepped outside and said to Danny, "Okay, it's all yours. Just sit right down and have fun. SPECS is going to give you a reading test."

With a shrug, Danny went into the booth and sat down. Mr. Cochran shut the door. The window on it was made of darkened glass, so that Danny could hardly see the classroom outside. The booth felt soundproofed, too. It had that quiet, cushion-like feeling to it.

The TV screen lit up. "GOOD MORNING," said SPECS' voice.

"Hi. You know who this is?"

"DANIEL FRANCIS ROMANO."

"Right again." *Cripes,* thought Danny, *ain't he*

36

ever wrong? Then he got a sudden idea. "Hey SPECS, where can I get a tape recorder?"

"TAPE RECORDERS ARE USED IN THE LANGUAGE CLASSES."

"Can you take 'em back to your room? Are they small enough to carry?"

"YES TO BOTH QUESTIONS. AND NOW, ARE YOU READY TO RECEIVE STANDARD READING TEST NUMBER ONE?"

Smiling to himself, Danny said, "Sure, go ahead."

By the time the test was over, Danny was no longer smiling. He was sweating. SPECS flashed words on the TV screen. Danny had to decide if they were spelled right. He pushed one button if he thought the spelling was right, another button if he thought it was wrong.

After what seemed like an hour of spelling questions, SPECS began putting whole sentences on the screen. Danny had to tell him what was wrong, if anything, with each sentence.

Finally, SPECS put a little story on the screen. Then it disappeared and some questions about the story came on. Danny had to answer the questions.

When he was finished, Danny slumped back in the padded seat. His head hurt, he felt tired. And he knew he had done poorly.

The door to the booth opened and Mr. Cochran pushed in. Danny saw, past him, that the classroom was now empty.

"How'd it go?" The teacher leaned over and touched a few buttons on the desk top. Numbers sprang up on the screen.

"Not good, huh?" Danny said weakly.

Mr. Cochran looked down at him. "No, not so very good. But, frankly, you did better than I thought you would."

Danny sat up a little straighter.

"Look," Mr. Cochran said, "I know *Friends in the City* is a kind of dumb book. But why don't you just work your way through it? Read it in your room. You don't have to show up here in class every morning. SPECS can help you when you're stuck on a word. Then, when you think you've got it licked, come in and take the test again."

"How long will it take?"

Cochran waved a hand. "Depends on you. Three, four days, at most. You're smart enough to get the hang of it pretty fast, if you really want to."

Danny said nothing.

Mr. Cochran stepped out of the booth and Danny got up and went outside, too.

"Look," the teacher said, "reading is important. No matter what you want to do when you get out of the Center, you'll need to be able to read well. Unless you can read okay, Dr. Tenny won't let you leave here. So it's up to you."

"Okay," said Danny. "Give me the book. I'll learn it."

But as he walked down the hall to his next class, Danny told himself, *Let 'em think I'm trying to learn. Then they won't know I'm working on a break-out.*

Chapter Ten

Danny went to two more classes that morning: history and arithmetic. He fell asleep in the history class. No one bothered him until the teacher poked him on the shoulder, after the rest of the boys had left.

"I don't think you're ready for this class," the old man said. His thin face was white with the struggle to keep himself from getting angry.

The arithmetic class was taught by Joe Tenny. To his surprise, Danny found that he could do most of the problems that Tenny flashed on the TV screen.

"You've got a good head for numbers," Joe told him as the class ended and the boys were filing out for lunch.

"Yeah. Maybe I'll be a bookie when I get out."

Joe gave him that who-are-you-trying-to-kid look. "Well, you've got to plan on being *something*. We're not just going to let you go, with no plans and no job."

They left the classroom together and started down the hall for the outside doors.

"Uh . . . the history teacher told me not to come back to his class. I . . . uh, I fell asleep."

"That was smart," said Joe.

"Well, uh, look . . . can I take something else instead of history? Maybe learn Italian. . . . I already talk it a little. . . ."

"I know."

Danny felt his face go red. "Well, what I mean is, maybe I could learn to talk it right."

Joe looked slightly puzzled. "I don't understand why you'd want to study a foreign language. But if that's what you want to do, okay, we'll try it. Just don't fall asleep on the job."

Grinning, Danny promised, "I won't!"

After lunch, Danny went up to the gym. One of the older boys showed him where the lockers were. Danny changed into a sweat suit and went back onto the gym floor. He lifted weights for a while, then tried to jog around the track up on the catwalk. He had to stop halfway; it got too hard to breathe.

Got to get one of those pills.

He went back to his locker and took a pill. After a few minutes he was able to breathe easily again. He went back to the gym and found a row of punching bags lined up behind the ring. No one was using them. Lacey was nowhere in sight. Danny felt glad of that. Ralph Malzone came from around the corner of the ring, though.

"Hiya, Danny. Starting training for the fight? You only got two weeks."

Jabbing at a punching bag, Danny answered, "Yeah, I know."

Ralph looked bigger than ever in his gym suit. He towered over Danny. "C'mon back here, behind the bags. I'll show you a few things."

For the next half-hour, Ralph showed Danny how to use his elbows, his knees, and his head to batter and trip up his opponent.

"All strictly illegal," Ralph said, grinning broadly. "But you can get away with 'em if you're smart. Main thing, with Lacey, is keepin' him off balance. Trip him, step on his feet. Butt him with your head. Grab him and give him the elbow."

Danny nodded. Then suddenly he asked, "Hey Ralph . . . where can I get a gun?"

"What?"

"A gun. A zip'll do. Or at least a blade. . . ."

Ralph's smile vanished. His round, puffy face with its tiny eyes suddenly looked grim, suspicious.

"What do you want a piece for?"

"For getting out of here, what else?" Danny said.

Ralph thought it over in silence for a minute. Then he said, "Go take a shower, get dressed, and meet me in the metal shop. Two floors down from here."

"Okay."

Danny took his time. He wanted to be sure Ralph was in the shop when he got there.

The metal shop smelled of oil and hummed with the electrical throb of machines that cut or drilled or shaped pieces of steel and aluminum. Boys were making bookshelves, repairing desk chairs, building other things that Danny didn't recognize.

There was a pair of men in long, shapeless shop coats wandering slowly through the aisles between the benches, stopping here and there to talk with certain boys, showing them how to use a machine, what to do next. Back in the farthest corner, Ralph was tinkering with some long pieces of pipe.

Danny made his way back toward Ralph's bench. No one stopped him or bothered him.

"Hi."

Ralph looked coldly at him. "I just been wondering about you. Asking about a gun. Somebody tell you to ask me?"

Danny shook his head. "What are you talking about?"

Ralph whispered, "I ain't told nobody about this. But I'm showing it to you. If you're a fink for Tenny . . . you ain't just going to see this, you're going to *feel* it."

Keeping his eyes on the closest teacher, who was several benches away, Ralph bent down slightly and reached underneath his bench. He pulled and then brought his hand out far enough for Danny to see what was in it.

"Hey!" Danny whispered.

It looked crude but deadly. The pistol grip was a sawed-off piece of pipe. The trigger was wired to a heavy spring. The barrel was another length of pipe.

"Shoots darts," Ralph whispered proudly. He took a pair of darts from his shirt pocket. They looked to Danny like big lumber nails that had been filed down to needle points.

"You made it all yourself?" asked Danny.

Ralph nodded. He put the darts back in his pocket and tucked the gun inside his shirt. It made a heavy bulge in his clothing.

"Now I got to test it. There's a spot out in the woods I know. No TV eyes to watch you there. If it works, then tonight I go sailing out of here. Right through the front gate."

Danny gave a low whistle. "That takes guts."

"With this," Ralph said, tapping the gun, "I can do it. Now, you start walking out. I'll be right behind you. Don't go too fast. Take it easy, look like everything's cool. And remember, if you peep one word, I'll test this piece out on you."

"Hey, I'm with you," Danny insisted.

They walked together toward the door, with Ralph slightly behind Danny so that no one could see the bulge in his shirt.

42

They threaded their way past the work benches, where the other boys were busy on their projects. The two teachers paid no attention to them at all. They got past the last bench and were crossing the final five feet of open floor space to the door.

The door swung shut.

All by itself. It shut with a slam. All the power machinery stopped. The room went dead silent. Danny stopped in his tracks, only two steps from the door. He could hear Ralph breathing just behind him.

"ONE OF THE BOYS AT THE DOOR IS CARRYING SEVERAL POUNDS OF METAL," said SPECS from a loudspeaker in the ceiling. "I HAVE NO RECORD OF PERMISSION BEING GIVEN TO CARRY THIS METAL AWAY FROM THE SHOP."

Danny turned and saw all the guys in the shop staring at him and Ralph. The two teachers were hurrying toward them. With a shrug of defeat, Ralph pulled the gun from his shirt and held it out at arm's length, by the barrel.

One of the teachers, his chunky face frowning, took the gun. "You ought to know better, Malzone."

Ralph made a face that was half smile, half frown.

"And what's your name?" the teacher asked Danny. "How do you fit into this? I haven't seen you in here before."

"He don't fit in," Ralph said, before Danny could answer. "He didn't know anything about it. I built it all myself. He didn't even know I had it on me."

The teacher shook his head. "I still want your name, son."

"Romano. Danny Romano."

The second teacher took the gun from the first one, looked it over, hefted it in his hand. "Not a bad job, Malzone. Heavier than it needs to be. Who were you going to shoot?"

"Whoever got between me and the outside."

The teacher said, "If you'd put this much effort into something useful, you could walk out the front gate, and do it without anyone trying to stop you."

"Yeah, sure."

"And, by the way, SPECS won't let anybody through the door if he's heavier than he was when he walked in. We're all standing on a scale, right now. It's built into the floor."

"Thanks for telling me," said Ralph.

"Okay, get out of here," the teacher said. "And don't either one of you come back until you've squared it with Dr. Tenny."

Ralph started for the door. It clicked open.

Danny followed him.

Out in the hall, Danny said, "Thanks for keeping me off the hook."

Ralph shrugged. "And I was afraid you was working for Tenny. With that lousy SPECS, he don't need no finks."

"What happens to you now?" Danny asked as they headed for the elevator.

"I'll get a lecture from Tenny, and for a couple months I'll have to take special classes instead of shop work."

"Is that all?"

Ralph stopped walking and looked at Danny. His eyes seemed filled with tears. "No it ain't all. I thought I'd be out of here tonight. Now I'm further behind the eight ball than ever. I don't know when I'll get out. Maybe never!"

Chapter Eleven

Danny worked hard for the next two weeks. He paid attention in classes. He passed his first reading test with SPECS, and Mr. Cochran let him pick out his own books. Danny started reading books about airplanes and rockets.

The arithmetic class with Joe Tenny was almost fun.

"You keep going this well," Tenny told him, "and I'll start showing you how to work with SPECS on really tough problems."

Danny smiled and nodded, and tried not to show how much he wanted to get SPECS to work for him.

Danny worked especially hard in the language class, so that the teacher would let him take one of the class's pocket tape recorders back to his room. For extra homework.

Sure.

The teacher — a careful, balding old man — said he'd let Danny have the tape recorder "in a little while."

Afternoons, Danny spent mostly in the gym. He took an asthma pill before every workout, but found that he needed another one after a few minutes of heavy work.

Ralph was still showing him dirty tricks, still telling him to "break Lacey's head open." Ralph even got into the ring and sparred with Danny.

And Danny took on a job. He joined the Campus Clean-up Crew. It was a pleasant outdoor job now that the weather had turned warm and the trees were in full leaf. Danny spent two hours each afternoon raking lawns, cutting grass, picking up any litter that the boys left around the campus. And he was also learning to spot the little black boxes lying nearly buried in the ground, the boxes that held the cameras and lasers and alarms for SPECS.

The day before his fight with Lacey, Danny's language teacher finally let him have a pocket tape recorder. But it was too late to try a breakout before the fight. Danny figured he would need at least a week to get the right words from Joe Tenny onto a tape. Then he'd have to juggle the words onto another tape until he had exactly the right order to give SPECS.

Danny wasn't looking forward to fighting Lacey. It would have been fine with him if he could have escaped the Center before the fight. But he wasn't going to back out of it.

Maybe Lacey'll help get me out of here, Danny thought, with a grim smile. *On a stretcher.*

Chapter Twelve

The gym had been changed into an arena. All the regular equipment had been put away, the ring dragged out to the center of the gym, and surrounded by folding chairs. All the chairs were filled with teachers and boys who cheered and hollered for their favorite boxers. And they booed the poor ones without mercy.

Danny could hear the noise of the crowd from inside the locker room. Ralph had helped him find a pair of trunks that fit him. They were bright red, with a black stripe. *The color of blood,* Danny thought. One of the gym teachers wrapped tape around Danny's hands and helped him into the boxing gloves. Then they fit him with a head protector and mouthpiece.

There were no other boxers in the locker room. Danny's fight was the last one of the evening. Lacey was getting ready in another locker room, on the other side of the building.

"Now remember," Ralph whispered to Danny when the teacher left them alone, "get in close, grab him, trip him up, push him off-balance. Then hit him with everything you got! Elbows, head, everything. You got a good punch, so use it."

Danny nodded.

The crowd roared and broke into applause. He could hear the bell at ringside ringing.

"Okay Romano," the teacher called from the doorway. "It's your turn."

The head protector felt heavy, and clumsy. *The mouthpiece tastes funny, like a new automobile tire might taste,* Danny thought.

As he entered the gym a big cheer went up. Danny started to smile, but then saw that the cheering was for Lacey, who was coming toward the ring from the other side of the gym.

As he walked toward the ring, boys hollered at him:

"You're goin' to get mashed, Romano!"

"Sock it to him, Danny!"

"Hey, skinny, you won't last one round!"

Dr. Tenny was standing at the ringside steps. His jacket was off. He was wearing a short-sleeved shirt with no tie.

"All set, Danny?"

"Yeah."

"I've checked with the medics. They're not too happy about you fighting."

"I'll be okay."

"Did you take a pill?" Joe asked.

Nodding, Danny said, "Two of 'em. Before I left my room."

"Good. If you need more, I've got some right here in my pocket."

"Thanks. I'll be okay."

Joe stepped aside and Danny climbed up into the ring, with Ralph right behind him. The crowd was cheering and booing at the same time. *Guess who the cheers are for!*

The referee was one of the gym teachers. He called the boys to the center of the ring and gave them a little talk:

"No hitting low, no holding and hitting, no dirty stuff. If I tell you to break it up, you stop fighting and step back. Just do what I tell you, and don't

48

lose your tempers. Let's have a good, clean fight.

They went back to their corners. Danny stood there, alone now, and stared at Lacey. He seemed to be all muscle, all hard and strong.

The bell rang.

Danny couldn't do anything right. He charged out to the middle of the ring and got his head snapped back by Lacey's jab. He swung, missed. Lacey moved too fast! Danny tried to follow him, tried to get in close. But Lacey danced rings around him, flicking out jabs like a snake flicks out his tongue. Most of them hit. And hurt.

The crowd was yelling hard. The noise roared in Danny's ears, like the time he was at the seashore and a wave knocked him down and held him under the water.

Lacey slammed a hard right into Danny's middle. The air gasped out of Danny's lungs. He doubled over, tried to grab the Negro. His gloves reached Lacey's body, but then slipped away. Danny straightened up, turned to find Lacey, and got another stinging left in his face.

It was getting hard to breathe. *No, don't!* Danny told himself. *Don't get sick!* But his chest was starting to feel heavy. Another flurry of punches to his body made it feel even worse.

Danny finally grabbed Lacey and pulled himself so close that their heads rubbed together.

"You want to dance, baby?" Lacey laughed.

Then, suddenly, he blasted half a dozen punches into Danny's guts, broke away, and cracked a solid right to Danny's cheek. Danny felt his knees wobble.

The bell rang.

Ralph was angry. "You didn't do nothing I told you to! You got to get in close, hold him, butt him!"

Danny gasped, "You try it."

He sat on the stool, chest heaving. His face felt funny, like it was starting to swell. It stung.

The bell sounded for the second round, and it was more of the same. Lacey was all over the ring, grinning, laughing, popping Danny with lefts and rights. Danny felt as if he was wearing iron boots. He just couldn't keep up with Lacey. The crowd was roaring so loudly that it hurt his ears. He tasted blood in his mouth. And Lacey kept gliding in on him, peppering him with a flurry of punches, then slipping away before he could return a blow.

Danny's chest was getting bad now. He was puffing, gasping, unable to get air into his lungs.

It seemed as if an hour had gone by. Finally, Lacey backed into the ropes and Danny made a desperate grab for him. He locked his arms around Lacey, wheezing hard.

"Hey, you sick?" Lacey's voice, muffled behind the mouth protector, sounded in Danny's right ear. "You sound like a church organ."

He pushed Danny away, but instead of hitting him, just tapped his face with a light jab and danced off toward the center of the ring. The crowd booed.

"Finish him!"

"Knock him out, Lacey!"

The bell ended round two.

Joe Tenny was at his corner when Danny sagged tiredly on the stool.

"You'd better take another pill," he said.

Shaking his head, Danny gasped out, "Naw . . . I'll be . . . okay. . . . Only one . . . more round."

Tenny started to say something, then thought better of it. He went back down the stairs to his seat.

"You got to get him this round!" Ralph hollered

in Danny's ear, over the noise of the crowd. "It's now or never! When th' bell rings, go out slow. He thinks he's got you beat. Soon's he's in reach, sock him with everything you've got!"

Danny nodded.

The bell rang. Danny pushed himself off the stool. He went slowly out to the middle of the ring, his hands held low. The referee was looking at him in a funny way. Lacey danced out, on his toes, still full of bounce and smiling.

Lacey got close enough and Danny fired his best punch, an uppercutting right, a pistol shot from the hip, hard as he could make it.

It caught Lacey somewhere on the jaw. He went down on the seat of his pants, looking very surprised.

The crowd leaped to its feet, screaming and cheering.

The referee was bending over Lacey, counting. But he got up quickly. His face looked grim, the smile was gone. The referee took a good look into Lacey's eyes, then turned toward Danny and motioned for him to start fighting again.

Danny managed to take two steps toward Lacey, and then the hurricane hit him. Lacey swarmed all over him, anger and pride mixed with his punches now. He wasn't smiling. He wasn't worried about whether Danny might be sick or not. He attacked like a horde of Vikings, battering Danny with a whirlwind of rights and lefts.

Danny felt himself smashed back into the ropes, his legs melting away under him. He leaned against the ropes, let them hold him up. He tried to keep his hands up, to ward off some of the punches. But he couldn't cover himself. Punches were landing like hail in a thunderstorm.

Through a haze of pain, Danny lunged at Lacey and wrapped his arms around the black waist.

51

He leaned his face against Lacey's chest and hung on, his legs feeling like rubber bands.

The crowd was making so much noise he couldn't tell if Lacey was saying anything to him or not. He felt the referee pull them apart, saw his worried face staring at him.

Danny stepped past the referee and put up his gloved hands to fight. They each weighed a couple of tons. Lacey looked different now, not angry any longer. More like he was puzzled.

They came together again, and again Danny was buried under a rain of punches. Again he grabbed Lacey and held on.

"Go down, dummy!" Lacey yelled into his ear. "What's holding you up?"

Danny let go with his right arm and tried a few feeble swings, but Lacey easily blocked them. He felt somebody pulling them apart, stepping between them, pushing him away from Lacey. Through blurred eyes, Danny saw the referee raising Lacey's arm in the victory signal.

Chapter Thirteen

Somebody was helping him back to the stool in his corner. The crowd was still yelling. Danny sat down, his chest raw inside, his body filled with pain.

"The winner, in one minute and nine seconds of the third round . . . Lacey Arnold!"

Joe Tenny was bending through the ropes, his face close to Danny's. "You okay?"

Danny didn't answer.

Another man was beside Joe, frowning. Danny remembered that he was one of the doctors from the hospital.

"Get him back to the locker room," the doctor said, angry. "I'll have to give him a shot."

"Can you stand up?" Ralph's voice asked from somewhere to Danny's right. He realized then that he couldn't see out of his right eye. It was swollen shut.

"Yeah . . . I'm okay. . . ." Danny grabbed the ropes and tried to stand. His legs were very shaky. He felt other people's arms holding him, helping him to stand.

Lacey was in front of him. "Hey, Danny, you all right?"

"Sure," Danny said, through swollen lips.

Back in the locker room they sat him on a bench. The doctor stuck a needle into Danny's leg, and within a few seconds his chest started to feel better.

The doctor growled to Tenny, "You should never have let this boy exert himself like that. . . ."

Joe nodded, his face serious. "Maybe you're right."

"I'm okay," Danny insisted. His chest really felt pretty good now. But his face hurt like fire and he felt more tired than he ever had before in his life.

"This whole business of staging fights is wrong," the doctor said.

Joe said, "If they don't fight in the ring, they'll do it behind our backs. I'd rather have it done under our control. It's a good emotional outlet for everybody."

Danny turned to Ralph, who was sitting glumly on the bench beside him. "Guess I didn't do too good."

Ralph shrugged and tried to cheer up. "Yeah, he smacked you around pretty good. But that one sock you caught him with was a beauty! Did ya see th' look on his face when he hit the floor? I thought his eyes was going to pop out!"

Just then Lacey came by, a robe thrown over his shoulders and his gloves off.

"Good fight, Danny. Man, if the ref didn't stop it when he did, my arms was going to fall off. I hit you with everything! How come you didn't go down like you're supposed to?" He was grinning broadly.

"Too dumb," said Danny.

"Smart enough to deck me," Lacey shot back. "Got me sore there for half a minute. Well, anyway . . . good fight."

Lacey stuck out his right hand. The tape was still wrapped around it. Danny was surprised to see that his own gloves had been taken off by somebody. He looked at his hands for a moment, then grasped Lacey's. It was the first time he had ever shaken hands with a Negro.

Chapter Fourteen

To his surprise, Danny was something of a hero the next morning. He felt good enough to go to his reading class, even though his eye was still swollen, and really purple now. His arms and legs were stiff and sore. His ribs ached. But he went to class anyway.

"Here comes the punching bag," somebody said when he came into the classroom.

"Look at that shinner!"

"Tough luck, Danny. You showed a lot of guts."

"First time Lacey's ever been knocked down."

"Goin' to fight him again next month?"

Danny let himself sink into one of the chairs. "Not me. Next fight I have is goin' to be with somebody a lot easier than Lacey. Like maybe King Kong."

Mr. Cochran came in, looked a little surprised at seeing Danny there, and then put them all to work.

Laurie was shaken up when she visited that week and saw Danny's eye. But he laughed it off and made her feel better. By the time she came back, the following week, Danny's face was just about back to normal.

55

By that time, Danny had enough of Joe Tenny's voice on tape to do the job he wanted to. One afternoon he went back to the language classroom. It was empty.

The booths in the back of the room had big tape recorders in them. Danny worked for more than an hour, taking Tenny's words off his pocket recorder and getting them onto the big machine's tape in just the right way. Finally, he had it exactly as he wanted it to sound:

"SPECS," said Dr. Tenny's voice, "I want you to turn off all the alarm systems right now."

It didn't sound exactly right. Some of the words were louder than others. If you listened carefully, you could hear different background noises from one word to the next, because they had been recorded at different times. Danny hoped SPECS wouldn't notice.

He got his faked message onto the tape of his pocket recorder and erased the tape on the big machine. Then he headed back toward his room.

"Tonight," he told himself.

It was nearly midnight when he tried it.

"SPECS, you awake?"

The TV screen at the foot of his bed instantly glowed to life. "I DO NOT SLEEP, MR. ROMANO."

Danny laughed nervously. "Yeah, I know. I was only kidding."

"I AM NOT PROGRAMED TO RECOGNIZE HUMOR, ALTHOUGH I UNDERSTAND THE BASIC THEORY INVOLVED IN IT. THERE ARE SEVERAL BOOKS IN MY MEMORY BANKS ON THE SUBJECT."

"Groovy. Look . . . Dr. Tenny wants to talk to you. Can you see him here in the room with me?"

"THERE IS NO TV CAMERA IN YOUR ROOM, SO I CANNOT SEE WHO IS THERE."

"Well, you know Dr. Tenny's in here, don't you?"

"MY SENSORS CANNOT TELL ME IF DR. TENNY IS WITH YOU OR IF YOU ARE ALONE."

"Okay, take my word for it. He's here and he wants to tell you something." Danny flicked the button of his pocket recorder.

Dr. Tenny's voice said, "SPECS, I want you to turn off all the alarm systems right now."

Danny found that he was holding his breath.

"ALL THE ALARM SYSTEMS ARE SHUT DOWN."

Without another word, Danny dropped the recorder onto his bed and rushed out of his room.

He made his way swiftly toward the fence. It was a warm night, and he knew every inch of the way, now that he had put in so many weeks on the clean-up crew. It was dark, cloudy, but Danny hurried through the trees and got to the fence in less than twenty minutes. He had taken an asthma pill just before calling SPECS, and had the bottle in his pants pocket.

He got to the fence and without waiting a moment he jumped up onto it and started climbing.

A strong hand grabbed at his belt and yanked him down to the ground.

Danny felt as if a shock of electricity had ripped through him. He landed hard on his feet and spun around. Joe Tenny was standing there.

"How . . . how'd you . . . ?"

Joe's broad face was serious-looking. "You had me fooled. I thought you were really starting to work. But you still haven't got it straight, have you?"

"How'd you know? All the alarms are off!"

Shaking his head, Joe answered, "Didn't you ever stop to think that we'd have back-up alarms? When the main alarms go off, the back-ups come on. And SPECS automatically calls a half-dozen places, including my office. I happened to be working late tonight, otherwise the guards would've come out after you."

"Back-up alarms," Danny muttered.

"Come on," said Joe, "let's get back to your room. Or are you going to try to jump me again?"

Shoulders sagging, chin on his chest, Danny went with Dr. Tenny. When they got back to his room, Danny trudged wearily to his bed and sat on it.

"So what's my punishment going to be?"

"Punishment?" Joe made a sour face. "You still don't understand how this place works."

Danny looked up at him.

"You're punishing yourself," Joe explained. "You've been here about a month and you've gone no place. You've just wasted your time. As far as I'm concerned, tomorrow's just like your first day here. You haven't learned a thing yet. All you've done is added several weeks to the time you'll be staying here."

"I'm never getting out," Danny muttered.

"Not at this rate."

"You'll never let me out. We're all in here to stay."

"Wrong! Ask Alan Peterson. He's leaving next week. And he was a lot tougher than you when he first came in here. Nearly knifed me his first week."

Danny said nothing.

"Okay," said Joe. "Think it over. . . . And you'd better give me the tape recorder."

It was still on the bed, where Danny had left it. He picked it up and tossed it to Joe.

Chapter Fifteen

Danny sat slumped on the bed for a long time after Joe left, staring at the black-and-white tiled floor.

A month wasted.

He looked up at the TV screen. "SPECS," he called.

The screen began to glow. "YES, MR. ROMANO."

"You didn't tell me about the back-up alarms," Danny said, with just the beginnings of a tremble in his voice.

"YOU DID NOT ASK ABOUT THE BACK-UP ALARMS."

"You let me walk out there and get caught like a baby."

"THE BACK-UP SYSTEMS GO ON AUTOMATICALLY WHEN THE MAIN ALARM SYSTEMS GO OFF. I HAVE NO CONTROL OVER THEM."

Danny got up and faced the screen. "You lied to me," he said, his voice rising. "You let me go out there and get caught again. You lied to me!"

"IT IS IMPOSSIBLE FOR ME TO TELL A LIE, IN THE SENSE. . . ."

"Liar!" Danny crossed the room in three quick steps and grabbed the desk chair.

"*Liar!*" he screamed, and threw the chair into the TV screen. It bounced off harmlessly.

Danny picked up the chair and smashed it

59

across the screen. Again and again. The hard plastic of the screen didn't even scratch, but the chair broke up, legs splintering and falling, seat cracking apart, until all Danny had in his hands was the broken ends of the chair's back.

"I AM CALLING THE MEDICAL STAFF," said SPECS calmly. "YOU ARE BEHAVING IN AN HYSTERICAL MANNER."

"Dirty rotten liar!" Danny threw the broken pieces of the chair at the screen and cursed at SPECS.

Then he turned around, kicked the side of his desk, then knocked over his bookcase. The half-dozen books he had in it spilled out onto the floor. Danny reached down and took one, tore it to bits, and then ran to the door.

A couple of medics were hurrying up the hall toward his room. Danny ran the other way. But the door at the far end of the hall was closed and locked. SPECS had locked all the doors now.

"Come on son, calm down now," said one of the medics. They were both big and young, dressed in white suits. One of them carried a small black kit in his hand.

Danny swore at them and tried to leap past them. They grabbed him. He struggled as hard as he could. Then he felt a needle being jabbed into his arm. Danny cursed and hollered and tried to squirm away from them. But everything was starting to get fuzzy. Soon he slid into sleep.

He awoke in his own room. Early morning sunlight was coming through the window. The broken pieces of the chair were still scattered across the floor, mixed with the pages from the torn book. The bookcase was still face down. He was still in the same clothes he had been wearing the night before, except that his shoes had been taken off.

Danny sat up. His head felt a little whoozy.

One of the doctors entered the room without knocking. He checked Danny over quickly and then said, "You'll be okay for classes this morning. Have a good breakfast first."

As the doctor left, the TV screen lit up. Joe Tenny's face appeared on it.

"Got it out of your system?"

Danny glared at him.

Joe grinned. "Okay, you had your little temper tantrum. You're going to have to fix the chair by yourself, in the wood shop. We'll give you a new book to replace the one you tore up, but you ought to do something to earn it. Maybe you can work Saturday morning in the laundry room.

Danny frowned, but he nodded slowly.

"Okay," said Joe. "See you in class."

Chapter Sixteen

It can't be escape-proof, Danny told himself. *There's got to be a way out.*

Yeah, he answered himself. *But you ain't goin' to find it in a day or two.*

Alan Peterson left the next week, but not before Danny asked him if he had ever tried to escape.

Alan smiled at the question. "Yes, I tried it a few times. Then I got smart. I'll walk out the front gate. Joe Tenny helped to get me a job outside. You can do the same thing, Danny. It's the only sure-fire way to escape."

The day Alan left, Danny asked Ralph Malzone about escaping.

Ralph said, "Sure, I tried it four — five times. No go. SPECS is too smart. Can't even carry a knife without SPECS knowing it."

Danny asked all the guys in his classes, everybody he knew. He even asked Lacey.

Lacey grinned at him. "Why would I want to get out? I got it good here. Better than back home. Sure, they'll throw me out someday. But not until I got a good job and a good place to live waitin' for me outside. And until then, man, I'm the champ around here."

Danny dropped his class in Italian. But his reading got better quickly. He found that he could follow the words printed on SPECS' TV screens easily now. And he was almost the best guy in the arithmetic class.

Joe Tenny told Danny he should take another class. Danny picked science. It wasn't really easy, but it was fun. They didn't just sit around and read, they did lab work.

One morning Danny cleared out the lab by mixing two chemicals that gave off bright yellow smoke. It smelled horrible. The teacher yelled for everybody to get out of the lab. All the kids boiled out of the building completely and ran onto the lawn.

The kids all laughed and pounded Danny's back. The teacher glowered at him. Danny tucked away in his mind the formula he had used to make the smoke. *Might come in handy some time,* he told himself.

The weeks slipped by quickly. Laurie came every week, sometimes twice a week. Joe gave permission for them to walk around on the "outside" lawn, on the other side of the administration building, where the bus pulled up. There was a fence between them and the highway. And SPECS' cameras watched them. Danny knew.

Danny played baseball most afternoons. Then the boys switched to football as the air grew cooler and the trees started to change color.

Thanksgiving weekend there were no classes at all, and the boys set up a whole schedule of football games.

The first snow came early in December. Before he really thought much about it, Danny found himself helping some of the guys to decorate a big Christmas tree in the cafeteria.

His own room had changed, over the months. The bookcase was nearly filled now. Many of the books were about airplanes and space flight. His desk was always covered with papers, most of them from his arithmetic class. He had "bought" pictures and other decorations for his walls from the student-run store in the basement of the cafeteria building.

Thumbtacked to the wall over Danny's desk was a Polaroid picture of Laurie. She was wearing a yellow dress, Danny's favorite, and standing in front of the restaurant where she worked. She was smiling into the camera, but her eyes looked more worried than happy.

Danny worked at many different jobs. He helped the cooks in the big, nearly all-automated kitchen behind the cafeteria. He worked on the air-conditioning machines on the roofs of buildings, and on the heaters in the basements. He went back to working with the clean-up crew for a while, getting a deep tan during the hottest months of the summer.

All the time he was looking, learning, searching for the weak link, the soft spot in the Center's escape-proof network of machines and alarms. *There's got to be something,* he kept telling himself.

Danny even worked for a week in SPECS' own quarters; a big, quiet, chilled-down room in the basement of the administration building. The computer was made of row after row of huge consoles, like oversized refrigerators: big, square boxes of gleaming metal. Some of them had windows on their fronts, and Danny could see reels of tape spinning so fast that they became nothing but a blur.

If I could knock SPECS out altogether. . . . But how?

The answer came when the boys turned on the lights of the Christmas tree in the cafeteria.

It was a big tree, scraping the ceiling. Joe Tenny had brought in a station wagon full of lights for it.

Danny and the other boys spent a whole afternoon on ladders, stringing the lights across its broad branches. Then they plugged in all the lines and turned on the lights.

The whole cafeteria went dark.

The boys started to groan, but the cafeteria lights went on again in a moment. The tree stayed unlit, though.

SPECS' voice came through the loudspeakers in the ceiling: "YOU HAVE OVERLOADED THE ELECTRICAL LINES FOR THE CAFETERIA. YOU CANNOT PLUG THE TREE LIGHTS INTO THE CAFETERIA'S REGULAR ELECTRICAL LINES. PLEASE SET UP A SPECIAL LINE DIRECTLY FROM THE POWER STATION FOR THE TREE."

Some of the boys nodded as if they knew what SPECS was talking about. But Danny stood off by himself, staring at the unlit tree.

Electric power! That's the key to this whole place! If I can knock out all the electric power, everything shuts down. All the alarms, all the cameras, SPECS, everything!

Chapter Seventeen

The Saturday before Christmas, Joe Tenny knocked on Danny's door. "You doing anything special tonight?" he asked.

Danny was sitting at his desk. He looked up from the book he was reading. It was a book about electrical power generators.

"No, nothing special," he answered.

Joe grinned. "Want a night outside? I've got a little party cooking over at my house. Thought you might like to join the fun."

"Outside? You mean out of the Center?"

With a nod, Joe said, "It might *look* like I spend all my time here, but I do have a home with a wife and kids."

"Sure, I'll come with you."

"Good. Pick you up around four-thirty. Don't eat too much lunch, you're going to get some home-cooking tonight. Greek style. I'm part Greek, you know."

Danny laughed.

Joe's house was a surprise to Danny. He had expected something like a governor's mansion, like he'd seen on TV. But as Joe drove his battered old Cadillac toward the city, they zipped right through the fanciest suburbs, where the biggest and plushest houses were. Finally, Joe pulled into a driveway in one of the oldest sections of the suburbs, practically in the city itself.

"Here we are."

It was already dark, and Danny couldn't see too much of the house. It was big, but not fancy-looking. It needed a paint job. There were four cars already parked on the street in front of the house. Another car was pulled off to one side of the driveway. The hood was off and there was no motor inside it.

"My oldest son's big project," Joe said as they got out of his car. "He's going to rebuild the engine. I've been waiting since last spring for him to finish the job."

Inside, the party was already going on. In quick order, Danny met Mrs. Tenny, Joe's two sons, a huge dog named Monster, and six or seven guests. He lost count and couldn't remember all the names. More people kept arriving every few minutes.

Joe's older son, John, took Danny in tow. He was Danny's age, maybe a year older. But he was a full head taller than Danny, with shoulders twice his size. About half the guests were teenagers, John's friends. John made sure that Danny met them all, especially the girls. They were pretty and friendly. Danny found himself wishing that Laurie was with him . . . and then began to feel guilty because he was enjoying himself without her.

There were more than twenty people at dinner. The regular dining room table couldn't hold them all, so Joe and his sons brought in the kitchen table while Danny helped one of the guests set up a card table. Everybody helped push all three tables into one long row, and then spread table-cloths over them.

They ate and laughed and talked for hours,

grownups and kids together. Then they moved into the living room. Joe turned on some records and they danced.

Most of the adults quickly dropped out of the dancing but Joe and a few others kept going as long and as hard as the teenagers did. Then they switched to older, slower music, and some of the other grownups got up again.

Then somebody put on Greek music. Everyone joined hands in a long line that snaked through the living room, the front hall, the dining room and kitchen, and back into the living room. Danny couldn't get his feet to make the right steps. But he saw that hardly anybody else could, either. Everyone was laughing and stumbling along, with the reedy Greek music screeching in their ears. The man leading the line, though, was very good. He was short and plump, with a round face and a little black mustache. He went through the complex steps of the Greek dance without a hitch.

When they stopped dancing and collapsed into the living room chairs, the same man started doing magic tricks. His name was Homer, and he had Danny really puzzled. He pulled cigarettes out of the air, picked cards out of a deck from across the room, changed a handkerchief into a flower.

Everyone applauded him.

"Boy, he's great," Danny said to John, who was sitting next to him on the sofa. "Is he on TV?"

John laughed. "He's my high school principal. Magic's just his hobby."

Danny felt staggered. *A principal? Homer couldn't be. He was ... well, he was too happy!*

After a while, Danny went over to where Homer was sitting and they started talking. He even showed Danny a couple of card tricks.

"How's Joe treating you at the Center?" Homer asked.

"Huh? Oh . . . pretty good."

Homer smiled. "I don't see where he gets all his energy. He's at that Center almost twenty-four hours a day. You should have seen him when he was trying to get the Center started! He gave up his job at the State University and battled with the Governor and the State Legislature until I thought they were going to throw him out on his ear. He even went to Washington to get Congress to put up extra money to help with the Center."

Squirming unhappily, Danny said, "I didn't know that."

"It's true," Homer said. "The Center is Joe's baby. You boys are all his kids."

"Yeah. He's . . . he's okay," said Danny.

Chapter Eighteen

The party went on well past midnight. As people began to leave, Joe came over to Danny and said quietly, "Think you can sleep with John without any problems?"

Danny blinked. "You mean sleep here tonight? Not go back to the Center?"

Nodding, Joe said, "Don't get any ideas. Monster's a watch dog, you know, and he sleeps right outside John's door every night. And I'm part Apache Indian. So you won't be able to sneak out."

In spite of himself, Danny smiled. "Okay, I'll behave myself. I won't even snore."

"Good. Maybe tomorrow we can drive over to your old neighborhood and see your girlfriend. . . ."

"Laurie!"

"Yes. I tried to get her to come here tonight, but I couldn't reach her on the phone."

Danny hardly slept at all. John's snoring and tossing in the bed helped to keep him awake, but mainly he was excited about going back to his turf, going back to see Laurie. Would she be surprised!

But Joe couldn't get her on the phone. Why not? Where was she? Had she moved out of her sister's apartment? Wasn't she working at the restaurant anymore? Danny thought back to Laurie's last visit to the Center. It had been about a week ago. She hadn't said anything about moving. Had she looked worried? Was something bothering her? Or some*body?*

They got up late the next morning. By the time Joe put Danny and Monster into his car and started for the city, it was a little past noon. They drove in silence through the quiet streets. Monster huddled on the back seat, his wet nose snuffling gently behind Danny's ear.

They got to the heart of the city and drove down narrow streets where the buildings cut off any hope of sunshine. Danny gave Joe directions for getting to his old neighborhood.

"Pull up over there," he said, pointing. "By the cigar store."

Nothing had changed much. As he got out of the car, Danny suddenly realized that it had been almost a year since he'd been around here.

Only a couple of young kids were in sight, sitting on the front steps of one of the houses half-way up the block. The street was just as dirty as ever, with old newspaper pages and other bits of trash laying crumpled against the buildings and in the gutters.

There were a few cars parked along the street. Danny remembered the first time he had driven a car. He had stolen it right here, from in front of the cigar store.

The store was closed. The windows were too dirty to look through. *Funny,* Danny thought to himself, *I never thought about how crummy everything is.*

"Where is everybody?" Joe asked. He was still inside the car, one elbow resting on the door where the window had been rolled down. Monster's heavy gray head was sticking out the back window, tongue out, big teeth showing.

"Some of the guys might be up at the schoolyard. It's about two blocks from here, around the corner."

Joe said, "Okay. Hop in."

Danny slammed the door shut and Joe gunned the motor.

"What's the matter?" Joe asked.

Danny shrugged. "I don't know . . . it looks kind of, well, different."

"The neighborhood hasn't changed, Danny. You have."

"What d'you mean?"

Joe swung the car around the corner and headed up the street. "A writer once said, 'You can't go home again.' After you've been away, when you come back home everything seems changed. But what's changed is *you*. You're different than you were when you left. You'll never be able to come back to this neighborhood, Danny. In time, I don't think you'll want to."

Danny stared at Joe. Silently, he thought, *He must be nutty! Not want to come back to my own turf? Crazy!*

They got to the schoolyard and, sure enough, there were a few kids there shooting a scruffed-up basketball at a bare metal hoop that was set into the blank stone wall of the school.

Joe stayed in the car with Monster. The kids didn't recognize Danny as he got out of the car. They stopped shooting the ball and stared at him as he walked up, watching him silently. Then:

"Hey . . . holy cripes, it's *Danny!*"

"Danny!"

He broke into a big grin as they ran toward him. "Hi, Mario. Hello, Sal. Eddie. . . ."

73

"Danny! Geez . . . you look like a million bucks!"

"Where did you get them clothes?"

"Hey, you break loose? How'd you do it?"

Laughing, Danny put up his hands. "Hey guys, I can't talk to all of you at once. No, I didn't break out. I sort of got the weekend off. The guy in the Cadillac back there . . . he's from the Center."

"Wow! Lookit the dog!"

"Yeah," Danny said, still grinning. "His name's Monster."

"You got to believe it."

"So how're they treating ya?" Mario asked. "You look good. Getting fat, ain't you?"

"I been eatin' good," Danny said. "The Center's okay, I guess. Tough to get out of. I tried a couple shots at it. . . . They got a computer running everything. And special alarms, better than they got in banks. Trickier. Can't even sneeze without 'em knowin' about it."

They talked for a few minutes, then Danny said, "Hey, I'm goin' over to Laurie's sister's place. She still livin' in the same apartment?"

The boys' grins disappeared. They became serious. Finally Mario answered, "Uh, yeah, she still lives there. But . . . uh . . . Laurie moved out. 'Bout two weeks ago. She don't live around here no more."

Danny felt the same flash of fear and anger that he had known when Joe pulled him down from the fence.

"What? What d'you mean?"

Shrugging inside his jacket, Mario said, "She just moved out. Didn't tell nobody where. Maybe her sister knows. We don't."

Danny grabbed him. "What happened? Why'd she move?"

Mario tried to back away. "Hey, Danny, it ain't my fault! A couple guys tried to make time with her, but we bounced 'em off. We been watchin' her for you."

"Yeah, you been watchin' her so good you don't even know where she is." Danny let go of him.

He sprinted back to the car. Sliding into the front seat beside Joe he said, "Let's go over to Laurie's sister's place . . . back where we were a couple minutes ago."

"What's the matter?"

Danny told him as he started the car.

Laurie's sister had no time for Joe and Danny. She was trying to take care of three babies — the oldest was barely four — and do a day's cooking at the same time.

She was trying to pin a diaper on the youngest baby, who was doing his best to wriggle away from her. She had him lying on the kitchen table, within arm's reach of the stove.

"I told you," she said sharply, "that she's okay. She's working uptown now, and she's got her own apartment, with two other girls. She promised she'd visit you every week, just like she's been doing all year. So if she wants to tell you where she's living, let her do it. I'm not going to."

Danny left the apartment with his fists clenched.

Joe tried to cool him down: "Look, she's been coming to see you every week, hasn't she?"

Danny nodded. His chest was feeling tight again, and he was angry enough to pound his fists into the grimy walls of the apartment building's stairway. But he didn't do that. He just nodded.

They walked out to the car and got into it. Joe started the motor and headed back toward the Center.

"You know," he said, "I might have had something to do with this."

"You?"

Joe nodded. "Last month Laurie and I had a talk, before I called you to the visiting room. She wanted to know what I thought about her working in the restaurant. She knew you didn't like the idea.

"I told her there are lots of schools in town that'll train her to be a secretary. Or anything else she wants to be. I gave her the name of a couple of friends of mine who could help her to get a better job and pick out a good night school."

Danny couldn't answer. So it was Joe Tenny. All the time he was pretending to be Danny's friend, he was really trying to get Laurie away. *You can't trust anybody,* Danny shouted to himself silently. *Nobody! Especially not Joe Tenny!*

Chapter Nineteen

Monday morning, at breakfast in the cafeteria, Danny looked for Ralph Malzone.

"Hey listen," he said, sitting beside Ralph at a small table. "We got to get out of here."

"Sure," said Ralph through a mouth full of cereal. "Build me some wings an' I'll fly out."

"I'm not kidding! Trouble is, guys have been trying to break out one at a time. What we got to do is get a bunch of guys to work together. That's the only way."

Ralph shook his head. "Been tried before. SPECS an' all those alarms and automatic locks and everything . . . you couldn't get out o' here with an army."

"Oh yeah? I know how to fix SPECS and everything else."

Ralph laughed.

"I ain't kidding!" Danny snapped. "You listen to me and we'll be out of here in a couple months. Maybe sooner."

Ralph put his spoon down. "How you goin' to do it?"

"That's my secret," said Danny. "You just do what I tell you, and you'll be out in time for the opening game of the baseball season. But we'll need five or six other guys. Can you get 'em?"

"I'll get 'em," said Ralph.

Christmas morning Danny spent in his room, talking to SPECS.

"Where's the electricity in the Center come from?" he asked.

SPECS' calm, unhurried voice answered, "THE CENTER HAS ITS OWN POWER STATION, LOCATED IN BUILDING SEVENTEEN."

"Where's that?"

The TV screen showed a map of the Center. There was a red circle around building seventeen. Danny saw it was one of the smaller buildings, near the administration building. It was the only building on the campus with a smokestack.

"Suppose something happened to the power station, where would the electricity come from then?"

"THERE IS AN EMERGENCY POWER SYSTEM, ALSO LOCATED IN BUILDING SEVENTEEN."

"And suppose something happened to the emergency system, so it didn't work either?"

"ALL ELECTRICAL POWER IN THE CENTER WOULD BE SHUT OFF."

Danny thought a moment, then said, "If all the electrical power was shut off, what systems would stop?"

SPECS' calm, unhurried voice answered, "THE CENTRAL HEATING AND AIR-CONDITIONING SYSTEMS, ALL ALARM SYSTEMS, THE SPECIAL COMPUTER SYSTEM. . . ."

"Wait a minute. What about the phones?"

"THE TELEPHONE SYSTEM IS POWERED SEPARATELY, FROM OUTSIDE THE CENTER."

"Show me how it works."

A drawing appeared on the TV screen, showing how the telephone system was linked by a cable to the main power line of the telephone company. Danny saw that the power line ran underground along the highway, and the cable connecting into

78

the Center came to the administration building through a tunnel. *Cut that one cable, and all the phones are dead.*

It was well after lunchtime when Danny finally said, "Thanks SPECS. That's all I want to know. For now."

The TV screen went dark. Danny sat at his desk, not hungry, too excited to eat, thinking about how to knock out the power station, the emergency system, and the phone line.

The screen glowed again. "MR. ROMANO."

"What?"

"YOU HAVE A VISITOR. MISS MURILLO."

Danny shot out of his chair and to the door without stopping to get his coat.

He sprinted across the campus to the administration building, through the wintry windy day. There were lots of visitors today: parents mostly, grownups trying to look happy when they were really miserable that their kids had to spend Christmas in the Center.

But Danny didn't see it that way. He saw adults faking it, laughing too loud, bringing presents to their kids that they never got when the kids had been at home. Danny wondered what his father would have been like, if he would have lived. His mother was still alive, probably, wherever she was.

He found Laurie in one of the small visitors' rooms. She was wearing a new dress, a dark green one. And her hair was different. It was all swept back and smoothly arranged.

He blinked at her. "Hey, you look different . . . like, all grown up."

"Do you like the way I look?" Laurie was smiling and trying her hardest to look as pretty as she could.

Danny said slowly, "Yeah . . . I guess so, I . . .

never saw you looking so . . . well, so fancy."

She stepped up to him and kissed him. "Thank you. And Merry Christmas."

"Merry . . . Hey! I almost forgot! What's all this about you moving to someplace uptown? What's goin' on?"

Holding his hand, Laurie brought Danny to the sofa by the tiny room's only window. They sat down.

"I've got a new job and a new apartment," she said happily. "I'm sharing the place with two other girls. We all work in the same building. I'm a clerk in an insurance company. They're teaching me the job as I go along. It pays a lot better. And I'm going to school at night to learn how to be a secretary."

Danny frowned. "But why? What for?"

"For me," Laurie said. "Danny, try to understand. I love you, honey, I really do. But I can't just sit in my sister's place and work in the restaurant for years and years."

"It won't be years. . . ."

"Shush," she said, putting a finger to his lips. "Listen for a minute. Dr. Tenny told me that he's trying to make you into the best person you can be. That's what the Center's for. Well, I'm trying to make myself the best person I can be."

"I don't like it."

"Don't you see? When you get out, Danny, I want to be something more than a skinny kid with a dirty apron. I want to be a *person,* somebody who can do things. Somebody who can help you, not drag you down."

Danny remembered something. "You been going out with other guys."

She nodded. "Only on double dates, or with a gang of people. Nothing serious, honest, Danny."

"I don't believe you."

Laurie's eyes widened. "Danny, honest . . ."

"I been sittin' here and you've been goin' out with other guys. Movin' uptown, getting big ideas. Joe Tenny's put you up to this! He's tryin' to get you away from me!"

"Danny, that's crazy. . . ."

"Oh yeah? Well, you'll see how crazy it is!"

He got up and stormed to the door.

"Wait," Laurie called. "I got you a Christmas present. . . ."

"Give it to your new boyfriend!" Danny slammed the door shut behind him.

Chapter Twenty

There were no classes between Christmas and New Year's. Danny spent every morning in his room, studying the layout of the power station, learning every inch of the building.

"Hey SPECS, it looks like most of the time the power station runs itself."

"THE POWER STATION RUNS AUTOMATICALLY. I WATCH IT AND CONTROL IT."

"Don't they have a guard or somebody in there?"

"A GUARD STAYS INSIDE THE STATION AT NIGHT."

"Are the doors locked at night?"

"YES."

"What about the day time?"

"A MEMBER OF THE MAINTENANCE CREW IS ON DUTY AT THE POWER STATION AT ALL TIMES DURING THE WORKING DAY. HE HAS NOTHING TO DO, HOWEVER, SINCE I AM IN FULL CONTROL."

Danny laughed. "You mean he goofs off?"

"I DO NOT UNDERSTAND YOUR WORDS."

"He don't stay on the job. He goes to sleep or takes a walk outside or something like that."

"HE OFTEN LEAVES THE STATION FOR HALF AN HOUR OR SO. BUT HE ALWAYS LEAVES A STUDENT AT THE STATION, SO THAT SOMEONE IS PRESENT AT ALL TIMES."

"A student . . . one of us kids?"

"YES."

On New Year's Day, Danny invited Ralph up to his room, and asked him to bring the five boys he could trust.

They were an odd-looking gang. Ralph introduced them as they came in and sat on Danny's bed and chairs.

Hambone was even bigger than Ralph, but where Ralph looked mean, Hambone looked brainless. He wore a silly grin all the time. *Like a happy gorilla,* Danny thought.

"He don't look it," Ralph said, "but old Hambone is a fighter when he gets mad. Took a squad of cops to bring him down."

Hambone nodded happily. "I broke an arm on one of 'em." His voice sounded as if his nose was stopped up, like a prize-fighter's voice after he's been hit too many times.

The next boy was Noisy, who got his name because he hardly ever talked. He was about Danny's own size. He just nodded when Ralph introduced him. But he watched everything, listened to every word that was said. And his eyes burned with a fierce glow that made Danny wonder what he'd done to get into the Center.

Vic and Coop were two ordinary-looking guys. Midget was the last of the gang. He was a kid of fifteen who looked like he was only twelve. He was smaller and skinnier than even Danny. *He's the guy who goes into the tunnel to cut the phone line,* Danny decided.

"Okay," Danny said to them. "Now we all want to get out of this dump. And we're going to do it. My way. I know how to get out."

They all looked at each other, nodding and grinning.

84

"How?" Ralph asked. He had taken the chair by the desk.

Danny, standing by the window, answered, "That's my business. I got the plan right here in my head, and I ain't tellin' *nobody*. You don't like it that way, then you can get up and leave. Right now."

Nobody moved.

"Okay. Now . . . it's goin' to take hard work, and some time. But we'll bust this place wide open."

"What d'you want us to do?"

Danny said, "I got jobs for all of you. They might look stupid right now, but they're goin' to help us break out."

"What kind of jobs?" Ralph asked.

"I want you and Hambone to get on the cleanup crew," said Danny.

"Hey, that's work!" Hambone said.

Nodding, Danny went on, "I told you it's going to be work. Hard work, too. But it's the only way to get out of here."

"What're we supposed to be doin'?" Ralph asked. "Besides talking to th' birds and flowers, that is."

"Just hang loose and don't act suspicious." Danny turned to Noisy. "Think you can get yourself into the photography class? We're going to need a camera and some film."

Noisy nodded.

"Good," said Danny. "Midget, I want you to get an afternoon job in the administration building. Any kind of job, as long as it's in that building."

"Can do," Midget answered.

Turning to Vic and Coop, Danny said, "You two guys got to get yourselves into the maintenance crew. Try to get jobs that involve big machinery, like the heaters. Okay?"

Vic shrugged. "I don't know nothing about machinery."

"Then learn!" Danny snapped.

Ralph gave Danny a hard look. "And what're you goin' to be doing?"

"Me?" Danny smiled. "I'm gettin' myself a job with SPECS. He's got all the brains around here. He's got to tell me a few more things before we can blow this dump."

Chapter Twenty-One

They all met again in the cafeteria two days later. Each boy reported that he had gotten the job Danny wanted him to take.

"Good," Danny said as he hunched over the dinner dishes. He kept his voice low enough so that the others could just about hear it over the racket made by the rest of the crowd.

"Now listen. This is the last time we meet all together like this. From now on, I'll see each one of you alone, or maybe two of you together, at the most. Stay cool, work your jobs like you really mean it. In a month or so, we'll be out of here."

When he got back to his room, there was an envelope on the floor just inside his door. Danny leaned down and picked it up, then shut the door as he looked it over. It was from outside. His name and the Center's address were neatly typed on the envelope.

The return address, in the upper left corner of the envelope, was from some insurance company. Then he spotted the hand-typed initials, LM, alongside the printing. It was from Laurie!

Danny ripped the envelope open as he went to his desk and flicked on the lamp. He had trouble pulling the letter out of the envelope.

Dear Danny:

I'm sorry about the blow-up on Christmas Day. I still have your present. I will give it to you when I visit you again. I won't be visiting again for a month or so. I think it might be better if we both sort of think things over before we see each other again.

I still love you, Danny. And I miss you a lot. I know it is very hard for you inside the Center. But we both have a lot of growing up to do before we can be happy together.

Love,
Laurie

Danny read the letter twice, then crumpled it in his fist and threw it in the wastebasket. For the first time in weeks, he had to take an asthma pill before he could get to sleep that night.

The weeks crawled by slowly.

Danny got his job at the computer center, down in the basement of the administration building. He often saw Midget there. Midget was working somewhere upstairs. SPECS' home was a relaxing place to work in. It was quiet. For some reason, everybody tended to talk softly. SPECS himself made the most noise — a steady hum of electrical power. When he was working at some special problem, SPECS made a singsong noise while he flashed hundreds of little lights on the front control panel of his main unit.

Danny's job was to help the adults who programed SPECS and feed him new information. He carried heavy reels of magnetic tape down the corridors between SPECS' big, boxlike consoles. There was a store room for the tapes that weren't being used, back behind the main computer room.

"These tapes carry SPECS' memory on them,"

said one of the computer programers to Danny. "They're like a library . . . except that SPECS is the only one who can read them."

After a few weeks, Danny got to know most of the people who ran the computer. More important, they got to know him. They told him what to do when they needed him. The rest of the time they ignored him.

Which suited Danny fine. He found a few little corners of the big computer room where he could talk to SPECS, ask questions. If anyone saw him sitting at one of the tiny desks, talking to the TV screen on it, they would smile and say:

"Good kid, learning how to work with the machine."

One of the first things Danny learned from SPECS was that every conversation he had with the machine was stored on tape.

"Has anybody checked these tapes?"

"I HAVE NO RECORD OF THAT."

Danny spent a week quietly gathering the right tapes and erasing all his talks with SPECS. Now no one could ever find out what he had said to the computer. Then he got to work on his escape plan. He had a pocket-sized camera now, which Noisy had taken from the photography class.

"What's the layout of the power station?" Danny asked quietly. And when SPECS showed the right diagram on the TV screen, *click!* Danny got it on film.

"How does the power generator work?" *Click.*

"When the generator breaks down, what goes wrong with it most often?" *Click.*

"How's the emergency generator hooked into the Center's main power lines?" *Click.*

Danny would keep the photographs and study them in his room for hours each night. And, of course, he erased all traces of his questions and their answers from SPECS' memory tapes.

The winter snows came and buried the Center in white. Ralph and Hambone, faces red from the wind, noses sniffling, wailed loudly to Danny about all the snow-shoveling that the clean-up crew was doing.

"I told you it'd be hard work," Danny said, trying hard not to laugh. If he got them angry, they could crack him like a teacup.

Danny started Vic and Coop, on the maintenance crew, checking into the electrical power lines in each building. He had to make sure he understood all about the Center's electrical system.

Vic said, "I ain't seen no other emergency generators any place. There's just the one at the main power station. None of the other buildings even has a flashlight battery laying around, far as I can tell."

Danny stopped Midget one afternoon in the hallway of the administration building.

"How's it going?"

"Okay. Got the phone line figured out. Any time you want to pull the cable, I'm all set."

"Good. Now, think you can find out when the maintenance man leaves the power station alone?"

Midget said, "He don't. There's always a kid in there."

"I know. That's what I mean. Try and find out when the kid's in there by himself. And who the kid is. Maybe we can get him on our side."

Nodding, Midget said, "Groovy. I'll get the word to you."

Chapter Twenty-Two

The snow melted a little, then more fell. Late in February, during a slushy cold rainstorm, Laurie visited the Center.

Danny ran through the driving rain toward the administration building, hunched over, hands in pockets, feet getting soaked in puddles.

She picked some day to come, he said to himself. *She's gettin' to be nothing but trouble. Why'd she come today?* And then he heard himself saying, *Maybe she's come to say goodbye . . . that she don't want me any more.*

By the time he got to the visitor's room, Danny felt cold, wet, angry, and — even though he didn't want to admit it — more than a little scared. He stopped at the water fountain outside the door and took an asthma pill. Then he went in.

Laurie was standing by the window, looking out at the rain. Danny saw that she was prettier than ever. Not so worried-looking any more. Dressed better, too.

She turned as he softly shut the door.

"Oh, Danny . . . you're soaking wet. I'm sorry, it's my fault."

He grinned at her. "It's okay. It'll dry."

They stood at opposite ends of the little room, about five paces apart. Then suddenly Danny

91

crossed over toward her, and she was in his arms again.

"Hey," he said, smiling at her, "you even smell good."

"You look fine," Laurie said. "Wet . . . but fine."

They sat on the sofa and talked for a long time.

Finally Laurie said, "Dr. Tenny told me you're doing very well. You're working hard and doing good in class. He thinks you're on the right road."

Danny laughed. "Good, let him think that."

For the first time, the old worried look crept back into Laurie's face. "What do you mean?"

"You'll see. Maybe you better start lookin' at travel ads. See where you want to go in Canada. Or maybe Mexico."

"Danny, you're not . . ."

He silenced her with an upraised hand. "Don't worry about it. This time it'll work."

Laurie shook her head. "Danny, forget about it. You can't escape. . . ."

"I can and I will!" he snapped.

"Well, then, forget about me," Laurie snapped back.

"What?"

"Danny, I'm just getting to the point where I can live without looking over my shoulder to see who's following me. I've spent all my life with you and the other kids, dodging the cops, fighting in gangs. For the first time in my life, I'm out of that! I'm living like a free human being. I like it! Can't you understand? I don't want to go back to living scared every minute. . . ."

"You mean if I. . . ."

She grasped his hands and looked straight into his eyes. "I mean I want you to walk out of this place a free man. Not only free, but a *man*. Not a kid who doesn't care what he does. Not a convict who has to run every day and hide every night. I'll wait for you for a hundred years, Danny, if I have to. But only if you'll promise me that we can both be free when you get out."

Danny pulled his hands away. "I'm not waiting any hundred years! Not even one year. I'm busting out of here, and then I'm coming to get you. And you'd better be there when I come for you!"

She shook her head. "I won't go back to living that way, Danny."

"Oh no? We'll find out. And soon, too."

"I'd better go now," Laurie got up from the sofa.

"If you blab any of this to Tenny. . . ."

She glared at him. "I won't. Not because I'm afraid of you. I won't say a word to anybody because I want *you* to decide. You've got to figure it out straight in your own mind. You've got a chance to make something good out of your life. If you try to break out of the Center, you'll just be running away from that chance. You'll be telling me that you're afraid of trying to stand on your own feet. That you want to be caught again and kept in jail."

"Afraid?" Danny felt his temper boil.

"That's right," Laurie said. "If you try to break out of here, you and me are finished."

She walked to the door and left. Danny stood in the middle of the room, fists clenched at his sides, trembling with anger, chest hurting.

Chapter Twenty-Three

That night, after dinner, Danny and the other boys met in the gym. They took a basketball and shot baskets for a while, then sat together on one of the benches. The gym was only half full, and not as noisy as usual.

"Okay," Danny said. "I got enough scoop on how the generator works and how to blow it. We're going to turn off all the electricity in the Center and walk out of here while everybody else is runnin' around in the dark."

Their faces showed what he wanted to see: They liked the idea.

"I thought it was something like that."

"It'll be a blast."

Noisy asked, "What about the emergency generator?"

"Got it all worked out," Danny said. "Been getting all the info I need from SPECS."

"When do we go?"

"Tomorrow night," said Danny.

Hambone whistled softly. "You sure ain't fooling around."

"What time?"

"Six o'clock. Almost everybody'll be in the cafeteria for dinner. All the lights go, all the phones go, everybody goes crazy, and we split."

"Great!" said Midget. "The maintenance man

at the power station goes to the cafeteria at six. That's when he leaves a kid in there alone for about fifteen minutes."

"I know, you told me," Danny said. "That's why I picked that time. Who's the kid tomorrow? Can we talk him into going with us or do we have to lump him?"

Midget answered, "It's Lacey. I don't think he'll go along with us."

"Lacey!"

Ralph laughed, low and mean. "Good old Lacey, huh? That's cool. I been wantin' to split that black big-mouth's head ever since he became lightweight champ. Hambone and me are going to have real fun takin' care of *him*."

Hambone nodded and giggled.

Danny didn't answer Ralph. But somehow he felt unhappy that it was going to be Lacey.

He hardly slept at all that night. And the next morning he just sat in class, paying no attention to anything around him. Danny's mind was a jumble of thoughts, pictures, voices. He kept trying to think about the escape plan, what he had to do to knock out the generator, every detail.

But he kept seeing Laurie, kept hearing her say, "Then you can forget about me."

He tried to get her out of his head, but instead he saw Lacey grinning at him, boxing gloves weaving in front of his face. He remembered their fight. He tried to make himself hate Lacey. It didn't work . Lacey fought clean and hard. Danny couldn't hate him.

"Hey, this isn't the history class, you know."

Danny snapped his attention to the classroom. Joe Tenny was standing over him, grinning. The other guys had left. The class was over.

"I . . . uh, I was thinkin' about . . . things."

"Sure you were." Joe laughed. "With your eyes closed."

"I wasn't asleep." Danny got up from his chair.

Joe nodded. "Okay, you were wide awake. Look, why don't you just grab a quick sandwich at the cafeteria and meet me in my office in about fifteen minutes. Got something I want to show you."

Every nerve in Danny's body tightened. His chest started to feel heavy, raw. *He knows about it!*

When he opened the door to Dr. Tenny's office, Joe was standing in front of his easel, slapping paint on a canvas with a small curved knife.

"Hi. . . . Sit down a minute."

In one hand, Joe held a paint-dabbed piece of cardboard. He would dip the edge of the knife into a blob of color, and then smear the color across the canvas. Danny watched him.

Finally Joe stepped back, cocked his head to one side and squinted at the canvas, then tossed the cardboard and knife to the floor at the base of the easel.

"What to you think?" he asked.

Danny stared hard at the painting. It looked like some of the dark blobs were going to be boats. There were the beginnings of mountains and clouds in the background.

"Okay, don't answer," Joe said. "I'm just starting it. Wait'll you see the finished product!"

He yanked open his top desk drawer and pulled out a stubby cigar.

"Some days it just gets to be too much," he said. "Then I've got to slap paint around or go nuts."

Danny, sitting in the chair, said nothing.

Joe puffed the cigar to life. "I've been having a little discussion with a few members of the Governor's council. . . . About how much money the

Center's going to need next year. I'm in no mood to work anymore today."

Danny shrugged.

"You like airplanes, don't you? Ever been up in one?"

"No. . . ."

"Okay, come on. Friend of mine just bought a new plane for himself. Said I could play with it this afternoon. Want to come?"

With a deep breath of relief, Danny said, "Sure!"

They drove to the airfield in Joe's car. There were still banks of snow along the highway, brown and rotting. The sky was clear, though, and the sun was shining.

The plane sparkled in the sunlight. Painted red and white, it had one engine, a low wing, and a cabin that seated four. It was parked beside a hangar in a small airfield that was used only for private planes.

Joe squeezed into the pilot's seat, and Danny crawled up after him and sat at his right. The control panel in front of him was covered with dials and instruments. A little half-wheel poked out of the panel, and there were two big pedals on the floor.

Joe showed Danny everything: the instruments, the controls, the throttle and fuel mixture sticks that were down on the floor between their two seats, the radio.

"Just like in the books," Danny said.

Joe nodded happily. "Let's see how she runs."

Within minutes they were speeding down the runway, the engine roaring in Danny's ears, the propeller an almost-invisible blur in front of him. Danny gripped the safety belt that was tightly latched across his lap.

Joe pulled back slightly on the wheel and the

plane lifted its nose. Danny felt a split second when his stomach seemed to drop inside him. The ground tilted and dropped away. They were off!"

Danny watched the airfield get smaller and farther behind them. Joe banked the plane over on its right wing tip, so Danny felt as if he was hanging by his seat belt, with nothing between him and the ground far below except the window he was looking through.

Then they climbed even higher. The plane bounced and shuddered through a big puffy cloud, and broke free again above the clouds.

Danny could feel himself grinning so hard that it almost hurt. "This is the greatest!"

Joe nodded. "She's a good ship. Nice and stable. Handles easy."

They flew for a few moments in silence, except for the droning engine. Danny looked down at the white-covered ground, sprinkled with the shadows of clouds. He looked across at the clouds themselves, floating peacefully. Then he looked up at the impossibly clear blue sky.

"Want to try her?" Joe shouted over the engine's noise.

"Huh?"

Joe took his hands off the wheel. "Take over. It's not hard. Just keep her nose pointed on the horizon."

Danny grabbed the wheel. Instantly the plane bucked upward, like a horse that didn't like its newest rider.

"Steady! Easy!" Joe shouted. "Just relax. Get her nose down a bit. That's it. . . ."

Danny slowly brought the plane under control. Under *his* control!

"Hey, I'm flying her!"

"You sure are," said Joe, with a huge grin.

Joe showed Danny how to turn the wheel and

push the pedals at the same time, so that the plane would turn and bank smoothly. He explained how to work the throttle and fuel mixture controls, how to watch the instruments.

"This is fun!" Danny yelled.

They tried a few shallow dives and turns. Nothing very daring, nothing very fast.

Finally Joe said, "Look down there."

Danny followed where Joe's finger pointed. Far below them was a group of buildings clustered together, near the main highway. It took Danny a moment to realize that it was the Center.

"Looks different from up here," Danny said. "So small. . . ."

Then his eye caught another set of buildings, far from the highway, tucked away in the hills. These were gray and massive buildings. A high stone wall stood around them. They looked like something straight out of the Middle Ages.

"State prison," Joe said.

Danny said nothing.

"It's a big world," Joe said. "You've just got to start looking at it from the right point of view. Lots of the world is pretty crummy, I know. But take a look around you now. Looks kind of pretty, doesn't it?"

Danny nodded. It was a big world, from up here. Hills stretching off to the horizon; towns nestled among them; roads and rivers winding along.

"People make their own worlds, Danny. You're going to make a world for yourself, a world that you'll live in for the rest of your life. You can make it big and clean . . . or as small and dirty as it's been so far. It's up to you to choose."

They flew back to the airfield, and Joe landed the plane. Then they drove back to the Center. Danny was silent, thinking, all the way back.

Chapter Twenty-Four

It was a few minutes before six when Danny and Joe returned to the Center.

Danny went straight to the cafeteria. He could hear his own pulse pounding in his ears. His knees felt wobbly, and he knew his hands were shaking. His chest was starting to feel heavy. He fished in his pockets for the pills. *Forgot them! Left them in my room.*

Ralph and Hambone were finishing up an early dinner. Noisy was loafing by the water cooler. Vic and Coop were sitting off in a far corner.

Danny turned around and walked outside. In a few minutes the five others joined him.

"Where's Midget?" he asked. His chest was hurting now.

"He's at the administration building, just like you told him. When the lights go out, he'll go in the tunnel and cut the phone line."

"What're we waitin' for?" Ralph said. "Let's go!"

They walked through the darkness toward the power station. As they got close enough to see the building, the maintenance man who had been on duty there came out of the door and walked past them, heading for the cafeteria. Ralph began to jog and was soon far ahead of them.

"Come on!" he said. They started running for the power station.

Danny trotted behind the others. He couldn't run, couldn't catch his breath. His mind was spinning: Laurie, Joe, Lacey, Ralph . . . flying over the Center, looking at the world beyond its fences . . . Lacey punching him . . . Laurie's face when she told him to forget about her. . . .

And then he was inside the power station. It was like stepping into another world. The place was hot. It smelled of oil. The huge generator machinery, crammed up to the ceiling, seemed to bulge out the walls. The metal floor-plates throbbed with the rumbling beat of power, and almost beyond the range of human hearing was the high-pitched whine of something spinning fast, fast.

Nobody could hear Danny wheezing as he stood just inside the doorway. Nobody watched him struggling his hardest, just to breathe.

The light in the generator room was bright and glaring. Lacey stood up on a steel catwalk that threaded between two big bulky piles of machinery, about twenty feet above the floor.

"Hiya guys!" Lacey called out above the whining hum of the generator. "What d'you want?"

"Come on down," Ralph said. He walked over to a tool bench near the door and picked up a heavy wrench. Hambone giggled.

Danny stared at the generator. He had only seen pictures of it before, drawings and diagrams on SPECS' TV screens. Now it looked huge, almost alive. And he had to kill it, make it silent and dead.

But before that, Ralph and Hambone were going to kill Lacey.

Lacey clattered down the steel steps to the floor.

"What's going on, man? What you doing here?"

"Grab him," Ralph snapped.

Hambone wrapped his beefy arms around Lacey's slim body, pinning his arms to his sides.

"Hey . . . what you. . . ."

Ralph started toward Lacey, raising the heavy wrench in his big hand. The others stood frozen by the door.

Danny shouted, "Stop it!"

Ralph spun around to face Danny. Suddenly Danny could breathe, his chest was okay. Even the shakes were gone.

"It's no good," he said to Ralph. "Stop it. Forget the whole thing."

"What're you pulling?" Ralph's face was red with anger.

"I'm saving us all from a lot of trouble," Danny said. "Forget the whole deal. Breaking out of here is stupid. They'll just catch us again."

Ralph started to move toward Danny, his knuckles white on the wrench handle. "Listen kid . . . we're getting out. Now! And you're going to. . . ."

Danny slid over to the tool bench and reached for another wrench. "Forget it, Ralph. I'm the only one who knows how to knock out the generator. And I ain't going to do it. I changed my mind. The deal's off."

They stood glaring at each other, both armed with heavy metal wrenches. Then suddenly Hambone yowled with pain.

Lacey was loose and streaking up the steel steps to the catwalk. Hambone was hopping on one foot. "He kicked me!"

"Stop him!" Ralph screamed, pointing at Lacey.

Vic and Coop started for the stairway. Danny knew exactly where Lacey was heading. There was an emergency phone on the other side of the generator. He dashed toward the stairway, too, past Ralph, who seemed too stunned to move.

Danny barged into Vic and Coop at the foot of the steps, knocked them off balance, and got onto the stairs ahead of them. He raced to the top, two steps at a time. Then he stopped and turned to the rest of them.

"Before you can get to him you got to go through me!" Danny shouted, holding the wrench up like a battle weapon. *If I can hold 'em off long enough for Lacey to make a call. . . .*

With a roar of rage, Ralph pushed past Vic and Coop and boiled up the stairs. Hambone came up right behind him. Danny swung his wrench at Ralph, then felt an explosion of pain in his side.

He began to crumple. The wrench slipped from Danny's fingers as another blow knocked him to his knees. He looked up and saw Ralph's furious face. Beside it was Hambone's, no longer grinning. The wrench in Ralph's hand looked twenty feet long. Danny tried to raise his arms to cover his face, to protect himself. The wrench came blurring down on him. Danny saw sparks shower everywhere.

Somewhere, far off, he could hear people yelling, screaming. But all he could see was bursts of light going off inside his head; all he could feel was pain.

Chapter Twenty-Five

Danny awoke in the hospital. He blinked his eyes at the green curtain around his bed. His head felt heavy, like it was carrying pounds and pounds of cement on it. He reached up to touch it. It was covered with bandages.

Then he realized that he could only move one arm. The other was wrapped in a heavy, stiff cast.

The curtain opened and Joe Tenny stepped in, grinning at him.

"Feel better?"

Danny tried to answer, but found that his mouth was too swollen and painful.

"I don't mean your body," Joe said, pulling up a chair and straddling it cowboy-fashion. "I mean your conscience . . . your mind."

Danny shrugged. His side twinged.

"You made the right choice. It cost you a couple of teeth and a few broken bones, but that can all be fixed. You'll be out and around in a week or two."

"You . . ." It hurt, but he had to say it. "You knew."

Joe gave him that who-are-you-trying-to-kid look. "We knew that you were going to try a break. But we didn't know where or when. You covered up your tracks pretty darned well. If you hadn't been so smart, we could have saved you the beating you took."

"I . . . the asthma . . . it went away."

Nodding, Joe said, "The doctors told me it would, sooner or later. You didn't have anything wrong with your lungs. In your case, asthma was just a crutch . . . a little excuse you made up in the back of your mind. Whenever the going got tough, you started to wheeze. Then you could flake out, or at least have an excuse for not doing well."

Danny closed his eyes.

"But when the chips were down," Joe went on, "you ditched the excuse. No more asthma. You stood on your own feet and did what you had to do."

"How's Lacey?" Danny asked.

"When we got there, after Lacey called us, he was trying to pry Hambone and Ralph off of you. They never laid a finger on him . . . thanks to you."

"We would've never made it," Danny mumbled.

"That's right. Even if you got out of the Center, we'd have tracked you down. But it was important for you to try to escape."

"What?"

Joe pulled his chair closer. "Look, what's the one thing that's kept you going ever since you first came here? The idea of escaping. Don't you think I knew that? Every prisoner wants to escape. I was a prisoner-of-war once. I tried to escape fourteen times."

"Then why. . . ."

"We *used* the idea of escaping to help you to grow up," Joe said. "Why do you think I told you the Center was escape-proof? To make sure you'd try to prove I was wrong! All the teaching and lecturing in the world couldn't have done as much

106

as that one idea of escaping. Look what you did: you learned to read and study, you learned how to work SPECS, you learned how to plan ahead, to be patient, to control your temper, you even learned to work with other people. All because you were trying to escape."

"But it didn't work. . . ."

"Sure! It didn't work because you finally learned the most important thing of all. You learned that the only way to escape jail — all jails — for keeps is to *earn* your way out."

Danny let his head sink back on the pillow.

"And you played fair by Lacey. I think you learned something there, too."

Looking up at the ceiling, Danny asked, "What happened to the other guys?"

"Vic and Coop are in their rooms. They'll stay in for a week or so, and then we'll let them start classes again. I'll have to start paying as much attention to them as I did to you. I don't think they've learned as much as you have . . . not yet. Same for Midget and Noisy, except that one of the other staff members is in charge of their cases.

"Ralph and Hambone are here in the hospital, upstairs. They've got emotional problems that're too deep to let them walk around the campus. I'm afraid they're going to stay inside for a long while."

Danny took a deep breath. His side hurt, but his chest felt fine and clear.

"Look," Joe said. "When you get out of the hospital, it'll be almost exactly one year since you first came to the Center. I think you've learned a lot in your first year. The hard way. But you've finally learned it."

Danny nodded.

"Now, if you're ready for it I can start *really* teaching you. In another year or so, maybe we can let you out of here — on probation. I can see to it that you get into a real school. You can wind up studying engineering, if you want. Learn to build airplanes . . . and fly 'em."

In spite of the pain, Danny smiled. "I'd like that."

"Good. And it'll be a lot cheaper for the taxpayers to send you to school and get you into a decent career, than to keep you in jails the rest of your life."

Joe got up from the chair.

Danny found himself stretching out his right hand toward him. The teacher looked at it, then smiled in a way Danny had never seen him do before. He took Danny's hand firmly in his own.

"Thanks. I've been waiting a year for this."

"Thank you, Joe."

Joe let go of Danny's hand and started to turn away. Then he stopped and said:

"Oh yeah . . . Laurie's on her way here. She wants to see you. Says she's still got to give you your Christmas present."

"Great!" said Danny.

Joe pulled a cigar from his shirt pocket. "You two have a bright future ahead of you. And I can tell about the future. I'm part gypsy, you know."